Alone I sing

(The pain is always there)

Written by

Alaa Zaher

The material and intellectual ownership of this book is subject only to the author, and any modification or copying of the contents of this book without the author's approval will be considered an infringement of the author's intellectual and material rights, as well as the personalities within the book from the author's inspiration, and has no connection to reality and if it is found in reality it is a coincidence. This is a work of fiction. Similarities to real people, places, or events are entirely coincidental.

Copyright © 2024 Alaa Zaher.

Written by Alaa Zaher.

Chapter One

I couldn't sleep that night; my mind was too preoccupied. I kept thinking deeply, repeating the same questions, filled with astonishment and wonder. **Had she left me!?** Had her feelings changed so quickly, or had she been pretending all those years? Over five years... really!!

No... impossible, she loved me. I always felt her passion and care. I'm not so naive to believe a false act. She was always beside me, encouraging me, witnessing her love for me many times. I realized the truth of her love through her treatment and saw her sincerity and loyalty in her sparkling black eyes. It's impossible for the eyes to lie.

I recall that morning at the university, it was my twenty-fourth birthday. We were at the beginning of our relationship... four months of amazement and madness—a short period, but I only believed that I loved her. A period of obsession and passion almost drove me insane due to the excitement I felt throughout that era, to the point where I didn't realize the chaos I was living in. I realized one thing during that phase: my great love for her to the point of madness. I wanted her from the beginning, it was clear to me. I always wanted to confess my love for her every day during that period, but I didn't for a reason I didn't understand. I was waiting, just waiting... maybe for the right moment, or maybe I was always succumbing to my fears. Indeed, I feared losing her.

On a beautiful sunny spring day, I sat on the wooden bench next to the lecture hall, waiting for the end of the class as per our agreed-upon schedule. I put on my earphones to listen to songs on my mobile phone, trying to kill the minutes of waiting and keeping my eyes fixed on the door to ensure I didn't miss her the moment she came out. I found myself immersed in the melodies of a romantic song filled with sadness and regret, talking about the suffering of a young man in love with a girl, but an unknown curse prevented them from being together. I was completely absorbed in the lyrics and my thoughts drifted far away, until I felt a light nudge on my back that startled me and brought me back from my reverie. I looked behind me, surprised. It was **her**... charming as always with her usual cheerfulness, covering her mouth to stifle her laughter.

I said to her: "Ah, **Maya**, it's you. Good morning."

She said, still laughing: "Good morning! What happened to you? I passed right in front of your eyes, and you didn't respond, unlike your usual self. So, I sneaked up behind you to scare you a little, and it seems I succeeded."

I said: "I didn't notice you passing by... I was lost in thought."

She replied, jokingly: "Thinking? Are you sad because you're getting older? ... Oh, I almost forgot, happy birthday."

I said with a smile: "Thank you. I thought you had forgotten my birthday."

I patted the empty spot beside me and said: "Please, **Maya**, have a seat."

She approached me with slow steps, then narrowed her eyes playfully and said: "Don't underestimate my abilities; I have a good memory."

Then she added in a soft voice after our eyes met: "Especially when it comes to birthdays; I never forget them."

Her face was radiant, extremely beautiful with her fair skin and blushing cheeks. I got lost for a moment in the details of her face. I was saying to myself, "Are you real? You are my dream girl. I've always waited for you and dreamt of you. You are perfect for me. I love you and every detail about you."

I spoke, almost unconsciously, as if I were still talking to myself: "Snow White."

She looked at me, puzzled, which made me snap out of my brief daze. I said: "You resemble her... **Snow White**, the character from the animated film with the seven dwarfs. And I added jokingly: I always said to myself, 'Where have I seen you before,' and now I've discovered the secret."

She tilted her head slightly backward, gave me a friendly look, and her cheeks turned even redder with embarrassment. Then she looked down and started fidgeting nervously. She seemed pleased with my compliment, so from that moment on, I started calling her "Snow White" whenever I had the chance. It was the nickname I used to pamper her, and she always reacted the same way as if it were the first time.

She sat beside me and asked: "Did I ever tell you why I was named **Maya**?"

I shook my head and said: "Is there a story behind your name?"

She answered yes and added: "My parents were confused about what to name me, so they left it undecided until my birth. Two days passed after I was born, and they still hadn't agreed on a name for me. The whole family was present after we left the hospital, and my father decided to resolve the matter by seeking my grandmother's advice. My grandmother is a wise woman who always has plenty of advice and wisdom, often enhancing her guidance with proverbs and sayings.

My grandmother went through a lot in her life, especially after she was widowed by my grandfather, who left her with young children to care for. She struggled greatly to raise them until they grew up. My grandmother laughed at my father's request and said: 'You don't need to think too much; the answer is simple and obvious. Look at the girl's face. I suggest we call her **Maya**.' The whole family agreed on the name and liked it, and since that day, I've been called **Maya**."

I smiled and said: "You've really made me eager to meet your grandmother, **Stella**. She must have many stories to tell us."

I paused for a moment, then added after observing her face: "Your grandmother is truly smart, **Maya**. The name suits you perfectly."

She laughed a little and turned her head to the other side. Then, silence fell for a few moments. I noticed the evident tension in her behavior. She was glancing left and right as if she wanted to tell me a secret.

I looked at her with concern and said: "What's wrong? Is there something bothering you?"

She stood in front of me as if gathering her strength and said: "I have a surprise for you. I brought you a gift for your birthday, but I'm afraid you won't like it."

Then she took something out of her coat pocket that I couldn't distinguish. She put both hands behind her back and extended her tightly closed fists in front of my face and said: "You have to choose one of my hands. Both contain a gift, and you'll get to have only one today."

I laughed at her childish behavior, to the point of guffawing. I stopped laughing when she adopted a serious expression.

I said: "Can you help me? It's hard for me to choose."

She pointed with her eyes towards her right arm and mockingly said: "No, I won't help you."

I was about to choose her left side, going against what she wanted, but I hesitated for fear of ruining her surprise. I pointed to her right hand with my index finger, feeling a bit nervous.

She slowly opened it, smiling playfully, and said: "This is your gift. It's a silver ring. I hope you like it. If it doesn't fit, we can go to the jeweler to have it adjusted. I made arrangements for that. Here, wear it. I want to see it on your hand."

Her fearful look was evident. I think she was worried she hadn't chosen a gift that matched my taste.

I took the silver ring and examined it, trying hard to hide my astonishment at her choice. I wanted to play the villain for a moment and make her doubt herself, but she didn't give me the chance to tease her, especially after I sensed her intense excitement. Only then did I express my admiration. The ring was truly beautiful, engraved with a crescent and a star on both sides and a shiny white hexagonal stone in the center. What intrigued me was that it matched my taste, especially after I tried it on and found it fit perfectly. However, it didn't take long before I noticed her left hand, which she still clenched tightly. She moved her arm behind her back immediately after my gaze lingered in an attempt to find out what she was holding.

She playfully pushed me with her other hand and said: "You're greedy. Didn't I tell you only one gift?"

I took advantage of her kindness and said smartly: "I want to know what's in your other hand. It's my birthday, and it's impossible for you to refuse my request."

Without my insisting, **she** extended her arm before my chest, surrendering. Her clenched fist trembled, and I felt the matter was serious. I looked at **her** blushing face and asked her to open her hand, but she didn't. I felt her body tremble after I gently held her hand and opened it. What was this?... Red ink lines drawn in her palm, a decorated heart with the words "I love you, **Mason**" written in the center.

Her trembling spread to my body. My heart pounded, and the world around me stopped. I felt a happiness beyond description, a joy and delight I wished would last forever. I thought to myself, "She feels the same way about me, but she was braver in expressing it. I was hesitant to confess." Her act removed the doubt and fear from my chest, and I gently kissed her hand.

I looked at her blushing face and said: "I love you too, **Maya**. You are engraved in my heart."

Her beautiful eyes sparkled with tears at that moment. We forgot about the passing students. I still remember the laughter from a group of girls walking by and glancing at us. Unlike my usual self, I didn't pay attention to what was happening around me. I was drowning in my lover's ocean, a stormy sea with massive waves that would surely destroy you if they didn't carry you safely to shore, even if you were a skilled swimmer.

She looked at me silently, and I saw love in **her** eyes, an honest gaze. I wished those moments would never end, a memory I could never forget for as long as I live. I realized one thing that morning: **Maya** reciprocates my feelings. I cannot be mistaken. I believe that **Maya** truly loved me.

We talked on the phone that evening for more than four hours. Four hours passed quickly, like four minutes. I didn't feel the passage of time. We talked about the details of our lives, our childhoods, desires, and dreams. We continued in the same vein after that day. We didn't just meet after classes but also exchanged text messages on the way home. In the evenings, we sometimes talked on the phone or chatted on Messenger. Because of **Maya**, I became addicted to social media. Even my childhood friend **Adrian**, a tech enthusiast and internet news buff, was surprised by how attached I had become to Facebook, when I used to advise him not to spend too much time using it.

We would chat for hours every day without getting tired or bored. After the day of confession, our bond grew stronger, escalating like a bird flying higher without encountering a turning point to change its course downwards. **She** was the best thing that happened to me, changing my life for the better. My smile returned, the one I lost after my mother passed away two years before I met **Maya**. My mother had a sudden heart attack, which took her life. The medical report said her heart was shocked due to a sudden change in temperature. She was alone at home on a hot day. Her heart rate increased when she turned on the air conditioner right after finishing housework, according to the specialist doctor. My mother had a weak heart and never complained of any illness before. That was her first health setback, and unfortunately, it took her life. The dear one left me and my father, who was in his mid-forties, and my brother **Damian**, who was three years younger than me. **Damian** was fifteen at the time. Since the incident, I have been very worried about him; he was more attached to her than I was, being the youngest and her favorite. Besides, he was the one who found her lying on her bed, her hands on her chest. After the one who filled the house with her care and attention was gone, the house became like a haunted house. I couldn't stay in it anymore, especially after my father remarried. I often spent the night at my close friend **Adrian**'s house. He was like a brother to me, and sometimes I slept illegally at the university dorm with my classmate **Owen**, who was another close friend. He was a great companion and friend throughout the years I spent at the university. **Owen** came from a simple family in the south of the country. I respected him greatly for his morals and good manners. As they say, he couldn't hurt a fly.

Due to his praiseworthy traits, the university dorm security turned a blind eye to my presence inside because of my friendship with **Owen**. He was loved by everyone and couldn't refuse a request. We met by chance in our first year at the university after the physics professor assigned us to the same practical work team, and we quickly became best friends, experiencing the good and the bad together.

After my mother passed away, my life and my family's live were turned upside down, especially since my father started talking less at home. I felt his great grief due to my mother's sudden absence, but his silence added to our pain—**Damian**'s and mine. His terrifying silence became a source of fear and concern for me, but there was nothing we could do. I was the one doing the house chores during that time, with **Damian**'s help.

On weekends, I dedicated Friday mornings to cleaning the house and washing the accumulated clothes. Despite all the efforts made, our house was in a miserable state. Occasionally, my youngest aunt **Zara**, who lived in a nearby city, would visit us to do household chores and cook. Thanks to her, I learned to cook many dishes that I later benefited from, and I soon started cooking for my father and brother whenever I was home.

After seven months since my dear mother passed away, and on a Friday morning, my aunt visited us to help as usual. After we almost finished the housework, she called me to be alone with her in the living room, seizing the opportunity of **Damian** entering the bedroom.

My aunt sat on the couch and started talking: "**My dear Mason**, come and sit next to me. I need you for something important, my boy."

For a moment, I felt fear and said: "What is it, aunt? Are you complaining about something?"

She replied: "No, I am fine. I need you for an important matter, and that's it."

I realized the importance of the matter from the seriousness on her face. I hurried and sat next to her as she requested.

I asked her: "What's the matter, aunt?"

She appeared hesitant, then began to speak: "We found a wife for your father, my son."

In truth, I wasn't surprised by what she said. I had understood for a while what my aunts were planning. I expected this moment but didn't expect it to happen so quickly. I knew this marriage was inevitable and that our house needed a woman to care for it, but not so hastily. I still saw my mother's presence in the house, and her scent still filled every corner. The wound of her loss hadn't yet stopped bleeding. If it were up to me, I would have refused this marriage immediately. I couldn't bear the idea of another woman taking my mother's place. I could never accept that, but there was no choice since it was my father's desire and interest. But it's hard to accept this hasty decision. I got up from my seat and said in anger: "Not now, aunt. The wound hasn't healed yet."

At that moment, a flood of emotions overwhelmed me, forcing my eyes to shed a stream of tears. I ran out of the house and found a quiet corner where I let my tears flow like a torrent. I didn't return home until the evening. Upon entering the house, my father met me, showing signs of concern.

He asked me: "What's wrong, my son? Why did you miss lunch?"

Friday was different as it was the only day we used to gather for lunch. After my mother's death, sitting at the table together became rare on other days.

I replied in anger: "I didn't feel hungry."

If I were in the same situation with my mother, sitting down to eat would be the first thing she would ask me to do. Then she would bombard me with questions and scold me out of worry and fear for me, but it's different with my father.

He took a deep breath and said: "Why did you turn off your phone? I was very worried about you. I was about to go out and look for you."

I lied and replied: "It's the battery, dad."

He gave me a look as if he was blaming me for my lie and said: "I know what happened this morning. Your aunt **Zara** told me everything."

I had no choice but to lower my head and wait for what was coming next. He raised his voice slightly and added: "I want you and Damian in my room in a little while, so go call your brother from outside. I saw him in the neighborhood with his friends a moment ago, and don't be late because I need to talk to both of you tonight."

We entered my father's room after I called **Damian**, who looked confused as to what was going on. He had a look of astonishment on his face, as if he didn't understand what was happening, unlike me, who knew the purpose of this family meeting. My father asked us to sit on the edge of the bed while he stood facing us as if giving a speech.

When **Damian** realized the topic was marriage, he was shocked and didn't move. I think he couldn't comprehend the idea. He remained in astonishment throughout the meeting. Most of my father's speech focused on how this issue had caused him sleepless nights and that making the decision wasn't easy. He stressed that we had to accept the situation as it was necessary.

He added: "I cannot allow you to live in such a state. I won't let you bear the burden of the house and sacrifice your studies. I am responsible for you, and it is my duty to provide suitable living conditions."

My mind wandered far away while he spoke. I realized then that this marriage was inevitable, and my objection would only bring more sadness and hardship to me and my family. My protest could be seen as selfish and cause disruption to my family's peace. I made a difficult decision within myself, but I wanted to end the meeting and relieve my father, who was straining himself to convince us. I raised my hand to speak.

My father paused in his speech, then looked at me and nodded, allowing me to talk. I confidently looked into my father's eyes and said: "I agree, father... I agree."

I noticed **Damian** watching me with suspicion and astonishment, while my father showed sadness on his face, contrary to what I expected.

After a few seconds of silence, **Damian** stood up, scratched his head with one hand, and said: "I agree too, father... I agree."

The day of the wedding arrived, or rather there was no wedding, as everyone said. We would bring the bride and that's it, without any celebration or fuss. My father's wife was divorced and didn't have children. Apparently, her infertility was the reason for her divorce, according to what I was told. I met her the day the marriage contract was signed. She asked about my well-being and studies. She seemed cheerful, and everyone attested to her kindness and good character. Despite that, I couldn't accept the idea of another woman replacing my mother. My mother, who passed away ten months ago, took all the love and compassion I had known throughout my life with her.

In truth, my father's wife, Vivian, didn't leave any duty unfulfilled. She seemed happy to live with us and served us joyfully. She always wore a smile, expressing her love and sympathy for us. But I couldn't live with her in the same house. I couldn't see her taking on my mother's role. Just thinking about it brought immense pain and sorrow to my heart. As a result, I avoided staying home for long, to escape the pain and misery.

Chapter Two

Meeting Maya during that phase of my life was a divine gift. I still remember all the details of that day when I visited the university library with my friend **Owen** to borrow a book. I was in my fourth year at the university but wasn't a frequent visitor to the library.

I walked behind Owen, noticing the changes since my last visit. The number of tables had increased, and there was a change in their arrangement. While I was lost in examining the transformation, I passed by the table where she was sitting alone, fully engrossed in her book, unaware of her surroundings. While she was lost in her book, I was captivated by her in a place where the air seemed to vanish and gravity faded in the face of her attraction.

While I was stunned by her spark, she continued to ignore me, bowing her head and giving me no attention. I was about to turn my head to continue my path and forget the magic touch that struck me when I felt a violent collision that produced a sound significant enough to catch her attention and make her look up to see what was happening. The sound was caused by my collision with **Owen**, who had suddenly stopped while I was walking. Unfortunately, I am slightly taller, and while **Owen** was hit on the back of his skull, I was hit on my nose, which I held immediately after the collision. I started to groan in pain, but my eyes remained on her. I forgot the pain as she stood up. I wasn't even listening to what my friend was saying. At that moment, all I remember is his concern for my condition while my heart raced at the rhythm of her steps towards me. Everything stopped suddenly when she turned and unexpectedly returned to her place in a state of panic and confusion. I didn't understand the reason for her sudden return. I was very disappointed and started talking to myself, asking... why did she turn back and not come? She was heading towards me... wait!... why is she in such a hurry and searching her bag? Did she remember something?

I realized what **Owen** was saying after looking at his face, feeling dizzy as if I were drunk. He urged me to sit in a chair a few steps away. I didn't know what was happening to me until I saw an unfamiliar arm approaching me. I immediately turned my eyes to the owner of the hand in confusion, while my hands didn't leave my nose. It was her, with a terrified face and a fearful look, trying to give me a towel and saying in a voice that settled in the depths of my mind: "Here you go, young man, take this towel, you need it." I didn't understand the purpose of using the towel until I removed one of my hands from my face to hold it and found my hand red. My nose was bleeding, causing me a light dizziness that knocked me to the ground. I caught the attention of a security guard who quickly took me to the university clinic.

I was very scared after losing a large amount of blood, but when I entered the clinic, it didn't take long before the nurse stopped the bleeding by placing sticks resembling bandages inside my nose and asked me to press on them and wait for about fifteen minutes for her to check the bleeding again. **Owen** held my arm with concern on his face while I pressed the piece of cloth the girl had given me tightly. After my condition improved, they asked me to rest and visit the hospital if the bleeding returned or if I felt dizzy. I wanted to leave quickly, hoping to meet the girl. I was praying that I would find her outside the clinic, waiting to check on me. I hurried out while the nurse was telling **Owen** to accompany me on the way. My spirits dropped when I didn't find her in the corridor with the people who accompanied me. I was looking forward to meeting her and talking to her, using the piece of cloth as an excuse to get closer to her. I was disappointed, especially after my friend and I returned to the library to see her again. Yes, I returned to the place where I saw her for the first time, hoping to meet her there again. I went back to the same spot after a debate with **Owen**, who was asking me to go rest while I made excuses to return the towel to its owner. The funny thing is that the cloth had been soaked in my blood, and returning it in that condition would have been considered foolish, something **Owen** kept repeating, but I didn't want to listen to him.

That evening, the dizziness subsided, and my condition improved a lot, but there was something inside me that I didn't understand, like a burden that afflicted me without any explanation. I realized later that it was the beautiful girl who occupied my thoughts and roamed the alleys of my mind. I asked myself... is this how someone who loves feels? And if so, is it love at first sight? Whatever it was, that evening, I was determined to meet her again to find the right explanation for all my questions.

I started frequenting the library whenever I had the chance. I think I visited it in two weeks more than the total visits I had made throughout my years at the university. I searched everywhere but to no avail, given the large size of the campus and the huge number of students. **Owen** noticed my frequent visits to the library and started joking with me after understanding what I was planning. He began calling me crazy and kept saying that I should find the towel Cinderella. I was like a madman... I would peek inside every hall I passed by and sneak a look through the windows of the classrooms, hoping to see her inside. I even started paying attention to every girl passing by, hoping to meet the girl who had stirred my thoughts.

On Thursday, after the morning study session, a group of my classmates and I hurried to one of the fast-food shops on campus to have lunch and return for the afternoon session. Getting food quickly during lunchtime was extremely difficult due to the high demand at that particular time. We had only two options: either stay hungry until all the classes were over or quickly eat before the afternoon session, which starts after a fifteen-minute break, or return late to the classroom, potentially facing unwelcome remarks from the professor. Usually, we assign one person from the group to buy food on behalf of the others to save time and make it easier for the shop owner. That day, it was my turn to buy the meals, and all my classmates knew it. Each person gave their order and money, and I went into the shop to buy the sandwiches. The place was crowded with students as usual, with loud voices, high laughter, and chaos in the queue... I remained focused on watching my turn to place the order because if I got distracted, someone intrusive would try to cut in line, causing me to be delayed and receive blame from my classmates later.

I was in that state when I heard a girl's voice at the front of the line saying to the vendor, "Two pieces of pizza, please." The voice seemed familiar, as if my ears had heard it before, but I couldn't recognize the owner. I looked through a small gap left by the crowd ahead of me, and the look froze me in place for a few seconds due to the astonishment I felt. I didn't expect to meet her in such a crowded place. I felt shy just thinking about the possibility of her refusing to talk to me in front of all these students. I started thinking of a proper way to communicate with her. A short distance separated us, with only a few people in between. I didn't know what to do, it was like an unexpected test that had to be passed without reviewing the lessons. I couldn't allow myself to miss such an opportunity. I snapped out of my small daze when she turned and excused herself to pass through the crowd to leave the shop. She passed by me, and I hoped she would at least give me a brief look to recognize me. That would have saved me the trouble of chasing her and eased my anxiety when starting a conversation. But alas, she passed me while looking down. I turned immediately behind her, trying to catch her attention, but to no avail. On the contrary, she started to increase her speed, as if she wanted to escape from me. If I hadn't hurried, I wouldn't have caught up with her. I was about to touch her shoulder to get her attention, but for a moment, I thought and feared that, as a girl and me being clueless about girls' thinking, she might misunderstand and scold me in public.

I did not call her at that time because I did not yet know the letters of her name. If I had called her "Hey girl," a group of girls would have turned to me, attracting the attention of passersby. This was exactly what I wanted to avoid. The looks of the people around me would have made me more embarrassed and tense.

I followed her and took two long steps to appear directly in front of her. Her reaction was to scream in fear. Suddenly, I found myself in a scene I did not envy. My fear of attracting some attention had turned into attracting all the attention. I felt all those eyes looking at us. I wished I could be an ostrich and bury my head in the sand.

I froze in my place once again, unable to comprehend what was happening and what I should do, all because of fear and embarrassment. Meanwhile, she raised her hands high and made a gesture with her eyebrows, trying to show her apology.

Maya tried to appear nonchalant and spoke first: "Hello, miss. I'm sorry for scaring you."

She did not respond immediately, letting silence prevail for a few moments while everyone anticipated what was happening between us, as if we were in an exciting scene from a dramatic movie. Everyone was silent, waiting for what was to come. At that moment, I felt my face heat up, and my heartbeats escalated. It was one of the most embarrassing moments of my life. We always laughed about it after we got together whenever we remembered that incident.

After what seemed like ages, she finally spoke and said: "Hello."

I paused for a moment, then continued the conversation: "Are you okay?"

She looked at me strangely and replied: "Yes, I'm fine. How can I help you?"

I leaned back, placing my hand on my chest, trying to show my surprise. I pointed to my face with my index finger and asked: "Really, don't you remember who I am?"

She answered: "No!"

I thought to myself: What have I gotten myself into? This is definitely a disaster, and it will end with me looking like a fool in front of the present crowd who were still eavesdropping on our conversation.

I said: "I am the one who had a nosebleed a few days ago, and I was at the library and..."

She interrupted me, saying: "Oh, right, I remember you now."

Then she bombarded me with questions: "How are you? Is the pain gone? Are you feeling better?"

Her interruption and initiative in the conversation really made me feel better. After her scream that drew attention, she was now diverting attention with her talk, making the spectators return to what they were doing before as if nothing had happened. This relieved a lot of pressure inside me. I managed to draw a shy smile on my face and said: "I'm fine, thank you. No need to worry, the injury wasn't that bad."

She smiled broadly, showing her bright white teeth, and said: "The bleeding was severe, and you lost a lot of blood. I'm glad you're okay."

I said: "I wanted to thank you for the help."

She replied: "No need to thank me. I didn't do much."

And added: "It was my duty, and anyone else in my place would have done the same."

I gathered my strength and dared to ask: "May I know your name, miss?"

She laughed and said: "Maya... my name is **Maya**."

I said: "**Maya**, nice to meet you. I'm **Mason**."

She replied: "Nice to meet you too."

I paused for a moment and then resumed talking: "Oh, I almost forgot... Your towel is still with me. I looked for you a lot in the library to return it, but unfortunately, I couldn't find you. I cleaned it, and I've been carrying it in my bag every day with the intention of returning it to you when I see you."

She tried to stifle her laugh, but even if she succeeded in hiding her facial expressions, her loud chuckle gave her away. From her gesture with her hand, I understood that she did not want the towel back.

I realized that this piece of cloth was my only chance to meet her and get closer to her, so I decided to use it as my trump card.

I raised my eyebrows in surprise and said: "You should take it back; it belongs to you. I left my bag in the hall, but I can return it later."

Maya spoke this time after managing to stop her laugh and said: "No... no need for that. You can keep it."

I shook my head firmly, confirming my insistence and said: "No, it's your trust, and it will return to you."

She smiled gently and accepted the reality, then said: "Okay, no problem. I'm late for my lecture now, which ends at three o'clock. I will meet you fifteen minutes after that at the library door. Is that okay?"

At that time, thoughts of my classmates, sandwiches, the teacher's scolding, and the resulting blame from my friends crossed my mind.

I answered enthusiastically: "Yes."

This clearly made her smile a kind smile.

I continued: "Okay, three-fifteen is a perfect time since my shift ends at three as well."

I added jokingly: "As for the place, I know it well now after visiting it so many times recently."

She said as she walked away: "Okay, see you later then. I'm late."

She hurried off, leaving me with a sweaty forehead, a pounding heart, and a wandering mind unable to grasp what was happening. I felt like my body was injected with excessive doses of adrenaline.

I cast an exploratory glance looking for my fellow students. I saw them waiting and talking among themselves without noticing what had happened to me. Our usual spot under the trees was a bit far. If they had witnessed what happened, I would have been nicknamed one of the lovers' names for weeks, maybe even months, along with their reprimand for my delay.

I rushed to place my order before anyone noticed me. Despite my efforts to make up for lost time, what we all feared happened. We received a ten-minute lecture from the professor about the importance of time and taking things seriously.

After the humiliating scolding, one of my colleagues whispered in my ear, jokingly, and said: "Don't worry, my friend. For the sake of food, I can endure all this disgrace."

I smiled and thought to myself: No, my friend, it's for **Maya** that I'll endure this disgrace.

I couldn't focus on the lesson throughout that evening. On the contrary, I barely stayed conscious without thinking. My heart was eager to see her again, and my mind imagined the details of the next meeting. I was lost in fantasy, expecting many scenarios and imagining various conversations. I prepared questions and answers intended to impress her.

Time passed very slowly. Every time I woke from my thoughts, I glanced at my wristwatch, whose small hand resisted reaching the number three. **Maya** returned to my mind, increasing my excitement and enthusiasm. This time, unlike usual, I didn't feel nervous; instead, I felt a strange confidence. For some reason, I was optimistic that the upcoming meeting would end well.

While I was floating in my thoughts and dreams, I heard the professor say, "You may leave now." Those words woke me up like an alarm clock. It was the most beautiful thing I heard that day from the professor since I had not focused on any other word he said, except for the part where he scolded us.

I grabbed my bag and quickly left the hall, bypassing some classmates on my way to the exit. I felt a hand pulling my shirt, and a familiar voice called my name, "Mason... Mason."

I turned towards the voice and asked: "What do you want, **Owen**?"

Owen spoke with a worried expression on his face: "What's wrong, my friend?"

I replied: "Nothing, I'm fine."

Owen: "Are you sure? You seem unusually quiet today."

I answered with a smile: "Everything is fine, my friend, but I have to go now. I'm in a hurry."

He clutched my shirt with both hands and said: "You won't leave before telling me what's wrong with you today."

Then he smiled mischievously, almost mockingly, as if he had realized something and added: "Does it have anything to do with Cinderella's towel?"

I removed his hands and said: "Yes, I found her. You need to let me go now so I don't lose her. I have an appointment with her in a few minutes."

Owen pushed me and showed signs of joy on his face, then said cheerfully: "Go quickly, she might be waiting for you now... Move fast."

I said nothing more and hurried towards the library, which was only a few minutes away. When I noticed **Maya** waiting for me from a distance, my heart began to pound. I couldn't explain my reaction. It was a strange mix of intense fear and a sweet feeling. The closer I got to her, the faster my heartbeats, while my steps grew slower. She was dressed in red and black. I approached her and said, without thinking or planning: "You look like a Coca-Cola bottle from afar!"

Her response was to bend over in laughter. Her laughter brought me some relief, which motivated me to follow with another clever remark: "I confirm for the second time; you look like a glass bottle, not a metal can." (Trying to express my admiration for her slender and captivating figure).

I noticed tears in her sweet eyes from laughing so hard. We quickly became synchronized in a way I couldn't have dreamed of. We talked and laughed so much that we forgot about the towel and started joking and making jokes. We stayed like that for over an hour without stopping or getting bored.

In a moment when I was about to speak, she looked at me in panic, widened her eyes, then looked at her phone and said: "I'm late, the last bus for students to my destination leaves in five minutes."

She added: "I lost track of time talking to you..."

The last sentence she said was the most beautiful thing I had heard in a while and was enough to make my day. My reaction was swift, and I said: "Let's hurry to the bus stop, it's not too late yet..."

She looked at me hesitantly and said: "I don't think so. It usually takes me at least ten minutes to walk to the bus stop."

I said seriously: "Who said you are going to walk? You will run, and I'll be with you."

She responded, her face filled with confusion: "Stop joking, I can't do that. I'm a grown woman now and stopped running since I was a little girl."

I took her bag in my hand and said: "Do I look like I'm joking?"

I started running and repeated: "Come on, let's run. You're wasting your chance. Come on, **Maya**, there's not much time left."

She chased after me, laughing, and said: "Come back, you crazy person, give me my bag. You're really insane."

Indeed, it was one of the crazy memories we shared together. We ran like fools, attracting all the attention while laughing and giggling, oblivious to the world around us.

Fortunately, we arrived just as the bus was about to depart. I handed her the bag and said, panting: "Here you go, the bus hasn't left yet. It's good you trusted me."

She took the bag, her face red and smiling, then said, breathing heavily: "Thank you, I really enjoyed meeting you."

I felt a surge of happiness from her words and said: "I also enjoyed meeting you and would like to see you again."

She put one foot on the bus step and turned to me, then answered cheerfully: "Sure, tomorrow at eight in the morning. I'm coming to attend a class in the hall next to the sports arena. You'll find me there."

I clenched my fist and raised my thumb up, indicating my agreement, and added: "Great, I'll be there."

The bus departed, and I stood in place for a while, hoping I wouldn't wake up from my dream. I couldn't believe how easily I harmonized with her. It was the beginning of an ideal relationship that I couldn't have wished for more.

The meeting was enough to unite two souls who were in desperate need of each other. This encounter led to a series of meetings, resulting in admiration, affection, and then love. Love that nourished my soul and revived it after it had been gasping for breath and awaiting its demise.

Chapter Three

As usual, I went to stay over at my friend **Adrian**'s house, just like every Thursday night; the next day was Friday, a weekend holiday. So, **Adrian** and I took the opportunity to stay up late, chatting and sometimes watching movies or discussing the latest in football. We've always shared a love for football, especially since we've supported the same team since childhood. We know every little detail about each other and consider each other as confidants.

I regard **Adrian**'s father, **Uncle Gabriel**, and his mother, **Aunt Grace**, as my own parents. They treat me like their son, and I always receive a warm welcome from them. I never felt like a stranger in their home; instead, I always felt like a family member. It may seem strange at first, but if you looked into our upbringing, you'd find that **Adrian** and I lived a childhood that closely resembled that of twins.

The same goes for **Adrian**, who is always welcomed in my family, especially by my mother, who used to call him "my son." I remember the day she passed away when everyone was consoling **Adrian** for his deep sorrow and continuous tears. I even heard whispers during the funeral, saying, "He must be the deceased's son," and they approached him to offer condolences.

Uncle Gabriel and **Aunt Grace** are delighted by my visit on Thursday evenings, especially since, in my absence, **Adrian** tends to go out and stay late in the neighborhood, which is not safe even during the day, let alone at night. **Adrian** argues that he works all week and needs this day to unwind, but his parents worry about him. That's why my presence at **Adrian**'s house every Thursday evening became almost necessary, providing a sense of calm and relieving the family's tension.

Adrian, who is a month and a half older than me, is the youngest among his siblings. He has an exceptionally intelligent brother named **Lucas**, who works as an assistant technical manager at a company specializing in electricity despite being under thirty. His sister, **Riley**, is five years older and is like the sister I never had. Both are married and live outside our city.

Adrian's obsession with technology and the internet led him to pave a unique path for himself. He dreamt of moving to a European country to work and live there for the rest of his life, possibly marrying a foreign girl. This dream drove him to form many online friendships with people from Europe, especially girls. In my opinion, the only positive aspect of this obsession was that it allowed him to master several languages and learn about various foreign cultures. This enabled him to work and excel easily in a prestigious hotel reception agency in the area.

Adrian's decisions are truly astonishing. One night, without any warning, he decided to drop out of school. He resolved to leave on his own accord without any pressure or justification. Despite his outstanding academic performance and his family's disapproval and my repeated advice to continue his education, he remained determined to follow through with his decision. He believes that school is a waste of time and will stand between him and his goals. Contrary to his wishes, I tried to convince him that attending university and obtaining advanced degrees was the best and easiest way to achieve his goals, but it was in vain; he never wavered from his decision.

As for me, I hadn't set any specific dream or goal for my future when I was young. I only knew that I had to complete my education and obtain a higher degree. That evening, we planned to watch an exciting action movie. Before that, we chatted in the room, as usual, while I turned on the TV.

Adrian began to tell me about one of the predicaments he faced that morning, which caused him to arrive late at work. A group of youths from a neighboring town tried to block the highway using burning tires to express their frustration over their dire living conditions and the poor state of their neighborhood. This action resulted in severe traffic congestion on the secondary roads. **Adrian** expressed his frustration and condemned these irresponsible actions, arguing that the only ones harmed by such behavior are the citizens themselves.

Unintentionally, I began to daydream about my meeting with **Maya** while **Adrian** continued to complain about his ordeal. In reality, I had spent most of the day thinking and daydreaming to the point where I feared it might damage my heart due to **Maya**'s repeated visits, which disturbed my composure and caused my heart to race.

I snapped out of my daze to find **Adrian** waving his hand in front of my eyes, his face showing both irritation and confusion.

He looked at me and said: "What's wrong with you? Are you okay?"

I looked at him confidently and replied: "Nothing, I'm fine."

Adrian: "Are you sure?"

I said: "Yes!"

He stood up as if he wanted to scold me and added: "You were daydreaming while I was talking. You didn't pay attention to what I was saying. I called your name several times, and you didn't answer!"

I said doubtfully: "You didn't call my name."

He denied it and raised his voice: "I swear I did it at least three times."

I showed expressions of surprise and said: "Sorry, my friend, I didn't notice."

He took a step closer and bent down to meet my face and said: "Won't you tell me what's on your mind?"

I didn't want to tell him then; I wanted to wait to see what would happen and then inform him about my situation in the coming days. But his inquisitive looks didn't allow me to keep it a secret for long.

I motioned for him to sit down and then narrated the events of the past days in detail from beginning to end. He was interested and eager to hear my story. He looked puzzled and asked me many questions, to which I answered shyly, as most of his inquiries were naive and embarrassing: "Is she beautiful? How old is she? Where does she live? Do you intend to marry her?"

That night, we didn't watch the action movie as planned. Talking about **Maya** took up all our time, and we didn't finish until after two in the morning.

Our meetings became frequent, and our relationship naturally strengthened over a short period. This brief time was enough to carve out a special place for **Maya** in my heart, imprinting her like a permanent tattoo in the most cherished parts of my being. I declared her my soulmate and beloved, though it was a secret between me and myself. In a short span, she ignited a revolution in my life—a sweet revolution whose flavor never ceased to satisfy my longing soul. I realized I was lost and helpless in the alley of love and infatuation without my permission. I became certain that I wouldn't wake from her revolution until I achieved my ambition and desire to spend the rest of my life with her by my side.

I became so accustomed to her presence that I couldn't even think of her absence. The mere thought of being away from her devastated me and awakened my deep sorrow. Talking to her and exchanging messages became part of my daily routine. Checking her letters and texts turned into a regular habit. Not an hour passed without me looking at my phone. Many people might criticize me for this state, and some might think I was overly attached to her. I would have been like them if I had put myself in their shoes. Those who haven't tasted the love and passion I felt at that time would never understand me. Love, dear sirs, is what tames the mightiest of people, humbles rulers and kings, and weakens the strong and mighty. So, imagine someone as weak as me, suffering from deprivation and loneliness.

I recall the day of **James**'s wedding, the son of my eldest aunt **Aurora**, on one of those beautiful spring days. The wedding was held at home, following the traditional way. My aunt **Aurora** lives in a small, picturesque town surrounded by many villages. Its charm lies in its inability to be classified as either a city or a large village. In the center, there is a famous market that attracts a large number of people from neighboring suburbs daily for work, trade, or shopping. It is 180 kilometers away from my city. I visited it many times in my childhood with my parents, especially during holidays and special occasions. I always enjoyed visiting my aunt's house and felt sad whenever I had to leave. I have a great companion there, **Oliver**, my aunt's son, who is almost the same age as me. He is **James**'s younger brother and a dear friend. He shared in most of my mischievous deeds in my childhood. We often recall our troubles and the predicaments we found ourselves in, laughing for hours at our foolish actions, especially our adventures with our neighbor **Uncle Benjamin** and our repeated entries into his orchard to steal walnuts from his large tree.

I didn't talk to **Maya** much that day. It was a busy and exhausting day, and I had to help manage the wedding, which distracted me from communicating with my "Snow White." In the afternoon, we set off in a large convoy of cars to fetch the bride, who lived about half an hour away. I rode in one of the cars with **Oliver** and two of his friends, creating an atmosphere of madness and joy. Then I remembered my phone, which I hadn't been apart from for this long in a while. I picked it up and checked the messages—one from **Maya** asking how I was.

I replied: "Hello, Snow White. I'm fine... The weather is nice here. I wish you were by my side at this moment. How are you?"

I waited only seconds until she replied: "I'm fine, feeling lonely because you've been busy lately, but I'm happy for you. What are you doing now?"

I replied: "We're on our way to fetch the bride. I eagerly await the day when I can bring you as a bride to my home."

She laughed long and added: "Hahahaha. I'm looking forward to that."

At that moment, **Oliver** and his friends asked me to put down the phone and join the celebration. I excused myself from **Maya** and promised to call her after fetching the bride and returning.

But something unexpected happened. After repeatedly using my phone to take pictures and record videos, the battery died. After returning with the bride, we immediately began serving dinner to the guests. The number of invitees was enormous—an immense crowd. We didn't stop for a moment, serving food, washing dishes, and cleaning the banquet area until it was about ten at night. I could barely stand when we finished all that.

Suddenly, I remembered my promise to **Maya**. I quickly called one of the neighbor's kids and asked him to take my phone and charge it at their house for a short time so I could make a quick call. Not a quarter of an hour passed before my patience ran out, and I asked him to return the phone. I quickly turned it on—the battery level was very low, but I could make a short call.

What's happening? The phone was out of control after a few seconds of turning it on. An enormous number of text messages and missed calls were received at once, all from **Maya**. I glanced at some of the text messages while anxiously waiting for the phone to recover from its near-seizure state. More than twenty messages, all from **Maya**, expressing her deep concern. There were thirty-eight missed calls from her. I hurriedly made the call and didn't wait long until she answered, her voice stuttering, which was unusual for her: "Hello!"

I spoke: "Hello, are you okay?"

Her voice trembled more, and she replied as if she didn't hear my question: "Where have you been all day? I was worried about you."

I answered with a reassuring tone: "I was busy all day; it was a hectic day." I started explaining what had happened, justifying my inability to contact her.

While explaining, I felt some confusion as she didn't utter a word for almost thirty seconds, unlike her usual behavior. I paused for a moment and then added: "Are you with me? Can you hear me?"

There was some silence, during which I could hear her breathing, which she interrupted by saying: "I thought... I thought you had an accident during the convoy to fetch the bride..." and suddenly she burst into tears. At first, I didn't understand what was happening, but after a few seconds, I realized the pain I had caused her. Hearing her cry shook my heart. I wouldn't allow anyone to make her sad, even a little, let alone myself being the source of her misery.

I listened to her sobs with remorse, trying to calm her down. After hearing her cry, I knew I wouldn't forgive myself for causing her distress that night. My happiness turned into sadness and pain. But, to be honest, deep in my heart, there was an indescribable feeling of delight and happiness. What drove this was experiencing the sensation of having someone who cares about you, cherishes you, and fears for your well-being.

I started asking myself, what is it about this love? It's truly strange, making you taste the bitterness of sadness and the sweetness of joy at the same time. I wished the call had lasted longer because that call wasn't enough to reassure her. But there was nothing I could do, so I had to leave, blaming myself. However, I realized one thing then: **Maya** and I are entangled with each other. Our relationship was no longer simple and easy. It went far beyond that. All creatures on Earth need oxygen to survive, except for **Maya** and me. In addition to the oxygen we breathe, we need each other to continue living.

Finally, a special day in my life arrived—the graduation day I had dreamed of since entering university. After five years of study and perseverance, six months of sleepless nights, and preparing the thesis, it was enough time to change my outlook on life significantly. I felt an evolution in my thinking and understanding compared to who I was before. I sensed maturity in my beliefs and wisdom in my mind that I wouldn't have achieved without going through the university period. I had unforgettable moments, met people I consider dear friends, experienced joy and sadness, laughed and cried. All these experiences made me proud to earn a master's degree in Renewable Energy and Energy Efficiency.

I spent the last week in the university dormitory to prepare the thesis with my partner, **Owen**, who shared every year of university with me. We managed to finish the final preparations two days before the presentation, allowing us to practice and memorize the introductions and paragraphs, especially preparing to answer the questions we anticipated from the professors who were members of the evaluation committee.

We didn't just face pressure from the professors. The presence of family members also placed a huge responsibility on us, particularly on **Owen**, who showed a lot of anxiety because he feared ruining things in front of his family, who had traveled a long distance from the south of the country to be there. He often told me that his family had high expectations of him, as he was one of the few in his family to have completed high school, let alone a master's degree.

The immense feeling of missing my mother frequently overwhelmed me during that period—a feeling that was unbearable at the most significant achievement of my life. My small family was there to support me, with my father, his wife Vivian, and my brother Damian present. Just seeing them near me boosted my morale. But my need for my mother was irreplaceable on such an occasion. I learned from her absence, which exceeded two and a half years, that she would always be eternally present in my heart. During that period, I realized that I would never get used to her absence. On the presentation day, my longing and missing her were overwhelming.

How could it not be, when I always imagined her accompanying me as I graduated from university, earning a prestigious degree that would make her prouder and raise her head high before everyone? Without my mother, my joy was incomplete. Tears unexpectedly flowed during the closing statement, unnoticed by everyone. Warm tears that everyone assumed were tears of joy, but they fell without my consent due to the deep sadness in my chest. I wiped them with my hand, but they kept falling.

It's beautiful to have a friend who understands and comprehends your situation. In that moment, **Adrian** hugged me to comfort me. If it weren't for him, I would have collapsed on the ground, crying like a small child in pain and unable to express his agony.

All I had left was to muster the courage and continue, ignoring my loneliness and pain and trying to avoid breaking down again.

One of the professors, the head of the evaluation committee, stood up. After praising our efforts and encouraging us to continue working hard, he announced the agreed-upon result by the committee, which was "Very Good." Joy filled the room as **Owen** and I received congratulations from everyone present.

Maya was there that day, sitting quietly at the far end of the hall throughout the presentation. I sensed from her behavior that she intended to keep a low profile and hide her identity from my family, as if she didn't want the spotlight on her. During that time, I glanced at her whenever I had the chance and found her sometimes smiling and sometimes giving me a thumbs-up, signaling her approval of my performance. Even after the result was announced, she didn't come forward to congratulate me amidst the chaos caused by the congratulations. She stood and watched from afar, joy evident on her face.

After things calmed down, I signaled her to come closer so I could speak with her privately.

We approached each other shyly, as if meeting for the first time. The eyes of the onlookers made us feel that way.

She initiated the conversation, saying in her usual modesty: "I'm happy for you and very proud of what you've achieved."

I looked at her admiringly, her face adorned with blushing cheeks, and said: "Thank you, my love. I'm also happy you stood by me and encouraged me wholeheartedly."

She tilted her head affectionately and said: "It's my duty. Congratulations, **Mason**."

I winked playfully and said: "No, you're mistaken. Congratulations to us."

She raised her eyebrows and asked in surprise: "To us… how so?"

I replied with a smile: "Yes, to us. Tonight marks the beginning of the countdown to our wedding date."

Noticing her face blushing with joy, I added: "I promise you, my beautiful, that I won't leave you no matter what. I plan to look for a job tomorrow and work hard to save enough money to propose to you next year and bring you as my wife."

A feeling of enchantment overcame me as her eyes sparkled and a sign of satisfaction appeared on her face. Then I said: "Do you agree?"

She answered joyfully with a melodious voice: "In fact, I've never been so sure of a decision as I am with this one."

The sweetness of her response made me doubt my hearing, so I asked again: "So, do you agree with what I said?"

She nodded affirmatively and said: "Of course, I agree. I'm with you, even in what you haven't said."

Her response bewitched me and shook my core. I felt a heavy burden lifted from my shoulders. I was a bit anxious since I hadn't discussed marriage with her before, even though I was almost certain of her agreement. I had planned that conversation many times and expected various answers but didn't anticipate such a comforting response. That response made me feel like the happiest man in the world that day.

Chapter Four

My hope of finding a decent job began to fade after two months of relentless searching. I submitted my resume to dozens of tech companies, but to no avail. Every morning, I woke up early like any regular worker and took public transportation to nearby areas, inquiring about industrial institutions. Usually, the response was that there were no vacancies available at the moment, and I was asked to leave my resume and wait for them to contact me if a position matching my specialization became available.

I arrived home around noon, after a long and tiring day of walking under the scorching summer sun in one of the nearby industrial zones. I was surprised when my stepmother, **Vivian**, greeted me with an unusually sad face.

I asked her, worried, my heart pounding with fear of something bad happening to the family: "What's the matter? Is everything okay?"

Vivian spoke in a low voice and gestured for me to sit down. "Please sit; I'll bring you lunch first."

I refused to sit and repeated my question: "I asked if everything is okay. Is there a problem?"

Vivian went to my father's room and returned with a piece of paper in her hand. She said: "Here you go... this concerns you. We received a call-up notice this morning regarding your conscription."

I sighed in relief for a moment, knowing that my family was fine. But soon, the promise I made to **Maya** came to mind. The summons required me to join the army in two weeks from that day to perform my national service duty for a full year. This would inevitably delay the engagement and, subsequently, the wedding date.

I took the summons, feeling deeply sad and angry. On top of not having a job, this was another burden added to my shoulders. I made a decision immediately, without deep thought. I resolved not to comply with the conscription order to avoid wasting more time, which would hinder achieving my set goal.

I intended to stick to my plan of marrying **Maya** as soon as she finished her studies. My father couldn't comprehend my decision, not knowing the motive behind my chosen path. He constantly urged me to reconsider my plan and go to the national service center within the specified time to avoid any future legal repercussions from the police and the national army. But all his attempts were in vain. Unfortunately, at that time, avoiding conscription was my only satisfying option.

Initially, **Maya** was greatly disappointed upon hearing the news of the summons, but as days passed, she began urging me to be patient and think rationally. She tried to convince me that it was just one year, which would pass quickly. She even went as far as to absolve me from my promise. My response was a firm refusal to all her attempts. I explained that the promise I made to her was a reflection of my own desire and not just a pledge to please her or to express my love for her.

That phase of my life was a turning point in my career path because it is difficult to employ someone deemed as a dissenter in the eyes of the state, especially in public institutions and companies. Achieving that was out of the question. Furthermore, I lacked professional experience to qualify for a prestigious position with a respectable salary that matched my degree. I hoped my name would not be added to the list of dissenters. I didn't have much time, as the law stipulates adding the person's name to the list after receiving three consecutive summonses.

My perspective on things changed since receiving that summons. I started planning to look for any legitimate job that could meet my needs, regardless of its nature. What mattered to me then was getting a job that would help me achieve my goals and reach my destination within the specified time, hoping for a later presidential pardon for national service dissenters, as is customary.

I announced my need for a job through all available means, whether through online platforms or by asking family members and acquaintances to mediate, as these are the prevalent methods in my society.

I was forced to abandon the principle of requiring a job in my field of study until further notice and to join a job that could provide me with the financial requirements to achieve my goals. Currently, my wish is to buy some time while waiting for a pardon that would grant me a national service card, a card that would facilitate obtaining a prestigious job in the future while I manage to achieve my desire to live beside my loved one.

Adrian was the only person who supported my decision from the beginning not to join the army. He, too, had taken the same approach as me. Since his youth, he never wanted to stay in the country. His biggest dream was to travel and live in a European city, trying his luck with foreign girls through technology, hoping to marry one and gain European citizenship. His constant interaction with foreigners was the primary reason he mastered many languages, thus gaining a decent amount of Western culture. He often suggested, sometimes even begged, that we plan to migrate together abroad.

I always rejected his proposals, arguing that his plans were just fantasies and fleeting whims. Beyond that, I allowed myself to advise him to stop thinking this way and encouraged him to stay with his parents to take care of them and gain their approval.

Adrian is known for his sharp intellect, despite not completing high school. In reality, he didn't believe in school education. His thinking was different from his peers. He wanted to migrate from the start. In the neighborhood, he's known as the young man obsessed with technology. Neighbors usually seek his help to fix their phone problems. He's fully aware of my deep attachment to **Maya**, but his support for my decision wasn't because of that. He believes it's a fleeting connection based on his own transient experiences, as he never stays in a romantic relationship for more than three months. My nature differs from his regarding relationships with girls. For me, it was my first romantic experience, whereas for **Adrian**, I'm certain he has lost count of the number of foreign girls he has dated.

Adrian is the keeper of my childhood and family secrets. He's the only person I trust and confide in. We understand each other's thoughts to the point of exchanging fleeting glances. I can even gauge his mood just by the tone of his voice without looking at his face. He's the first friend I ever made. I don't even remember the day I met him, as he was present wherever my memory takes me.

One evening, while I was with **Adrian** in his room watching an important match in the Champions League, his father entered after knocking.

He stood at the doorway and spoke with his hand still on the doorknob: "Hello, boys. How are you?"

I adjusted my lying position out of respect for him and replied: "We're fine, **Uncle Gabriel**. We're doing great."

Adrian's voice cut through mine, saying: "Come in, Dad. Sit and watch the match with us. It's an exciting game."

Uncle Gabriel waved his hand, refusing: "No, I didn't come to watch football. I want to talk to **Mason** about something important."

Anxiety gripped me, and I said, frightened: "Is everything okay, uncle? Is something wrong?"

Uncle Gabriel smiled as he approached and placed his hand on my shoulder to reassure me. "Don't worry, my boy, there's nothing to be concerned about," he said, before sitting next to me and squeezing my shoulder.

"I heard from my wife that you're looking for a job, and over the past few days, I've been inquiring among my friends about any opportunities. Today, I received news from a friend about a job offer in a neighboring city. I'm not sure if you'll accept it, so I wanted to consult you first. This position doesn't require any academic qualifications or intellectual skills; on the contrary, it demands some physical ability. But on the other hand, it offers a respectable salary. I know it's not the job of your dreams, but it's an opportunity you should seize while you search for a position that suits you, especially given the difficulty of finding a job these days."

I felt a mix of emotions and thought to myself, "This is my lucky day." I was overjoyed to hear the news, and without asking for any further details, I eagerly agreed. I was filled with excitement and determination to overcome all obstacles to achieve my desired goals and fulfill the promise I made to my beloved **Maya**.

Uncle Gabriel immediately contacted his friend to inquire about the job's conditions and location. The workplace was only a few kilometers from my home. The next day, I went to inquire about the nature of the job and discovered that it was in a large wholesale fabric store, one of the largest and most famous fabric stores in the area.

My role involved unloading goods from trucks arriving from the port, arranging them in designated areas, and loading the goods into customers' vehicles upon sale. Simply put, the offered job position was that of a porter. Despite the societal disdain for that title, I didn't care due to my urgent need for money. The motivating factor for this job was the convincing salary that would meet my needs.

Arranging the goods according to their types in designated areas and organizing them in layers required climbing ladders, which was considered dangerous and involved significant effort and concentration.

There weren't many workers, only four of us, all performing the same tasks. Surprisingly, everyone was new to the store, with the most experienced worker having only three months of experience. When I inquired about the lack of seasoned porters, some said that many people couldn't endure the job's hardships, often ending up with back pain and injuries. Some even fell from the ladder.

There was also a famous incident where a worker died on the way to the hospital after falling from a height of ten meters and hitting his head. Although it happened a decade ago, it still deterred young people from working in this particular store, despite the decent salary.

After hearing all this, I felt some hesitation and fear. But I quickly realized that my coworkers weren't following proper methods for lifting heavy loads and didn't pay attention to safety and prevention measures.

I discovered that their negligence and lack of care were the primary reasons for the daily injuries and strains. I had to research online to learn about safety measures and proper lifting techniques. I then took the initiative to teach my colleagues the safety principles I had learned.

As weeks passed, I improved in my work and became a valuable member of the store, gaining some muscle mass along the way.

The store owner, **Uncle Sebastian**, was an elderly man over seventy-three years old, a self-made person who had built his fortune on his own. He worked a lot despite his age, but the hard work had worn him down, and he recently started making many mistakes, especially in calculations. He continued to work, waiting for his only son to return from Canada after completing his studies, so he could help manage his father's assets.

Working in the store, which resembled a warehouse, was very interesting. It required some techniques and experience to make things easier, especially during holiday and wedding seasons when the demand for fabrics increased, putting extra pressure on the four workers.

I saw **Uncle Sebastian** as a kind and generous person who usually considered the employees' circumstances. He doubled the wages on difficult days due to the extra work and effort, giving everyone their due without delay or complaint. He took into account the workers' situations as long as each person was serious about their work.

However, he had another side, where he dealt harshly with the lazy and didn't hesitate to fire anyone who slacked off or took their work lightly. At the same time, he rewarded and compensated those who worked diligently and efficiently. He cared a lot about the workers' health and safety, given the rough nature of the job. He never missed a day without asking about everyone's well-being. If someone was absent, he would call to check on them. He encouraged us to rest when tired. Personally, I saw him as a good and righteous person and held him in high regard, just like all the other workers and customers who dealt with him honestly and faithfully.

One day, we were busy during the last hours of work, about to finish unloading a container of fabric from a truck, intending to arrange each type on its designated shelf in the store's warehouse. I suggested a new work method to my colleagues, forming a human chain. The idea was to reduce the long-distance travel with heavy loads by dividing the distance between us into four equal parts. Each person would cover a specific section, passing the load to the next person. The last person would place the fabric rolls on the ground near the ladders, forming a large pile.

After unloading all the goods, we started another phase, dividing the distance again, but this time on the ladders. Two workers climbed the ladder and securely tied themselves with safety belts designed for high areas. Another worker stayed at the bottom, carrying the cylindrical fabric rolls a short distance up the ladder, while the fourth worker received the load from the employees on the ladder and placed it on the shelf.

This method significantly reduced risks. Within a short time, everyone noticed a marked decrease in injuries and back pain. We managed to make the tasks more organized and efficient, reducing the time needed to unload shipments compared to before. For us, the porters, the level of fatigue decreased significantly, and we became more energetic and active, leading to abandoning the idea of resignation.

Uncle Sebastian noticed the rapid improvement in work quality over the past few weeks. One evening, he requested my presence in his office after finishing the fabric arrangement. I was surprised by his request, as he usually only summoned employees to his office on Thursday evenings to pay their weekly wages. It was a Monday, so something was up.

I headed to the office, my mind occupied with thoughts about the invitation. I knocked on the closed door, watching **Uncle Sebastian** through the upper glass part as he was engrossed with his calculator and accounting ledger.

He raised his head towards me and said: "Come in, **Mason**, sit down."

I greeted him, then walked toward the wooden chair and sat.

He returned the greeting, then bowed his head back to his ledger, saying: "Give me a few moments to finish the remaining calculations... It won't take long."

I reassured him: "Don't worry, uncle, take your time. Calculations require a lot of concentration."

He raised his eyebrows after glancing at me, closed the ledger, and said: "I know you have a good educational background, but I'm not sure what your field of study is. Speaking of calculations, I want to ask you a simple question: Are you good at math?"

I smiled, shrugged, and pointed to my chest with both hands. "Of course, I graduated from a technical field that requires skill in math and general calculations."

He nodded slowly and then asked, narrowing his eyes: "How long have you been working with us exactly?"

I replied: "Just one more week, and it'll be six months."

After pushing the ledger aside and placing the pen on the desk, he asked: "Do you want to continue working with us, or has the hard work exhausted you?"

I answered while scratching my scalp: "Yes, I want to continue working. I really need the job."

Uncle Sebastian spoke with a serious expression: "I need you for a specific task... or rather, a mission. I'll explain my intentions to you so you fully understand. I want you in one of the important positions; this position is critical in our business. Most of our economic transactions depend on it. I want you to manage all store statistics, including overseeing and maintaining records of all commercial transactions—both buying and selling—as well as managing the store's inventory and planning and executing orders for goods before the stock runs out. Most importantly, I don't want a single penny to go missing. Now, I need a clear answer... Are you capable of doing all this?"

He added, interrupting me before I could answer, pointing his finger at his head: "Oh, I almost forgot something important. You will receive a 20% salary increase for your service."

Initially, I was very enthusiastic, but after analyzing the situation, I realized the immense responsibility I had been entrusted with. I understood from **Uncle Sebastian**'s words that he wanted some rest and was now delegating most of his responsibilities to me in the store. He would now only conduct periodic checks on my work and that of the other employees, as well as personally handle the banking transactions. However, I couldn't pass up such an opportunity—I had to seize it and establish my presence in a field I knew little about.

I responded with the same seriousness, showing my appreciation for the magnitude of the task: "First, I thank you for your generous offer and for trusting me. But at the same time, I understand the huge responsibility you're placing on my shoulders. I agree, but I have a few conditions."

Uncle Sebastian was surprised by my response and leaned back in his chair before asking me to list my conditions.

I began listing my demands on my fingers: "First, I need an office and a computer specifically for work. Second, a software related to inventory management and commercial transactions must be acquired and installed on the computer. Third and finally, I request a 30% increase in my current salary."

Uncle Sebastian laughed and said: "I understand the third demand, but I don't quite get the first and second ones. I also worry about the high cost of the software you're requesting."

I then convinced him of the necessity to keep up with the times and that the era of ledgers and paper was over. The current situation required keeping up with technology, as it played a crucial role in the advancement of industries and commerce in general, making transactions easier and ensuring effectiveness and quality in work. I also explained that the cost of the software was minimal, and there was no need to worry about it.

He finally agreed to my conditions, except for the increase, where we settled on a 25% raise.

As expected, I faced significant challenges initially, as I had to start from scratch. First, I had to understand everything recorded in the ledger, then input the data into the software to create a database on solid and accurate foundations.

After work hours, I would rest briefly at home before delving into learning about management and economics by reading books in the field and watching educational videos online. I also exhausted my neighbor, **Nathaniel**, with questions to benefit from his extensive experience in inventory management, as he worked as an inventory manager at a well-known company. Thanks to him, I managed to learn all the features of the software installed on the computer.

I also faced some difficulties with customers initially, needing some time to gain each one's trust. It wasn't easy at all; everyone asked me to recount multiple times before printing the invoice, doubting its accuracy. But I didn't succumb to such pressures; instead, I re-did the work several times with a willing attitude.

In less than a month, all the store transactions were as precise as clockwork. Nothing happened without being integrated into the software. I managed the store with greater ease and efficiency than before. **Uncle Sebastian** acknowledged the correctness and validity of my thinking and regretted not considering using technology earlier. For example, when dealing with a single customer, the time difference between creating a handwritten invoice and a computer-printed one could exceed five minutes. Five minutes may not seem long, but during busy periods and increased work pace, it was enough to clear a line of anxious customers.

Chapter Five

I woke up to the sound of a notification on my phone, alerting me to a text message. I had planned to sleep in late on Friday morning after spending Thursday night at home, which was unusual for me. I wanted to take advantage of the weekend to rest and relax on the only day I didn't work. But lately, I had become accustomed to waking up early, perhaps because my biological clock had programmed itself to wake me up at the same time. I glanced at my phone and found a message on Messenger from my beloved **Maya**, saying:

"Good morning, sweetest **Mason**. Happy Birthday! I wish you a long life, and I hope to be by your side for the rest of it."

I had forgotten about my birthday, as I had grown used to doing in recent years. I hadn't celebrated my birthday with family or friends for over a decade, so this day had become like any other for me. My thoughts wandered, contemplating the curse of time that passes quickly. More than three years had passed since my first meeting with **Maya**—over a thousand nights since our relationship began, and yet I remembered every detail of our memories together as if they had happened only a few weeks ago.

I replied to her message: "Good morning, filled with happiness, to the most beautiful **Maya**. Thank you so much for your wishes as always. I apologize for the millionth time for forgetting your special occasions while you never miss mine. I promise I won't forget next time."

She responded after a few seconds: "Don't worry, my dear. I've forgiven you. Don't trouble yourself over it. I know you well and know that you do everything you can to make me happy. You're doing what you should and more, so don't sweat the details."

At that moment, an idea crossed my mind. Remembering her birthday, I sent her this message:

"Your birthday coincides with the summer holiday in about four months. How about I bring my family and propose to you on that day to make up for ruining it last time?"

She didn't take long to express her joy, sending several red hearts and a smiling emoji with heart-shaped eyes. She said: "It would be the best birthday gift I've ever received. You can't imagine how happy your proposal makes me."

Then she added: "But I don't want to pressure you. Don't rush your decisions just to make me happy."

I answered enthusiastically: "Nothing is too much for my Snow White. Besides, carrying out this proposal would make me happy too."

We spent the whole day talking about planning and coordinating the engagement details. I wanted to fulfill all her wishes to give her the engagement of her dreams. We discussed the topic through text messages for hours, during which I stayed in bed until lunchtime without noticing. Meanwhile, she was texting me and helping her mother with household chores. We exchanged messages in an atmosphere of joy that words cannot fully describe.

While chatting with her, I sensed the excitement in her due to my sudden proposal. I told her that I needed to talk to her father first. I planned to meet and discuss it with him regarding his daughter. I asked her to give me his phone number when the time for the engagement approached so I could arrange the meeting appropriately. She accepted most of my suggestions with innocence and open-mindedness, and I was delighted that I would finally meet her family after hearing so much about them.

Maya's house was about thirty kilometers away from mine. If it weren't for the university that brought us together, the likelihood of us meeting would have been extremely slim. Her family consists of five members, but currently, she lives alone with her father, **Uncle Wyatt**, and her mother, **Aunt Elena**. She has a brother, **Noah**, seven years older than her, who lives in the United Kingdom. He is married to an Irish woman and recently had a beautiful baby girl. She also has a sister named **Sana**, three years younger than **Noah**, who got married not long ago and lives with her husband, a navy soldier, in a historic city in the west of the country. **Maya** is the youngest member of her family, which explains the affection and pampering she receives.

Her father holds a special affection for her compared to her siblings, especially after her older sister **Sana** got married. After thinking and hesitating for hours, I finally decided to bring up the engagement topic with my family. It was difficult for me to directly discuss it with my father, so I decided to seek the help of my stepmother, **Vivian**, to act as an intermediary between us. **Vivian** was delighted and supportive when she heard the news. She reassured me by informing me that my father had previously expressed his desire to help me settle down, which added more joy and reassurance to my heart.

That same day, after dinner, I sat with a group of neighborhood friends, discussing politics and the latest developments in the country. I stopped listening to one of my friends' discussions because I received a phone call from my father. After answering, he asked me to come to the house urgently. From his tone, I gathered that **Vivian** had talked to him about the matter. I was surprised that she had done her part so quickly. I rushed into the house, feeling both anxious and embarrassed. I found **Vivian** at the entrance, and she asked me to go to my room where my father was waiting.

I entered and greeted him. He responded with a serious and firm expression, increasing my anxiety. He asked me to sit next to him for a conversation. Initially, he told me that he had been wanting to bring up the topic of marriage for some time and expressed his happiness that I was thinking about starting a family and settling down.

My father expressed his concern about my frequent nights away from home, which he considered an undesirable habit. He looked at me firmly again and bombarded me with a series of questions. The first one he asked, after intertwining his fingers, was whether I was ready for marriage and if I had fully understood the responsibilities.

He was worried about my ability to meet the family's needs, particularly regarding housing. Buying a house in my country is almost an unattainable dream, so we would need to purchase a small place to settle in, which would not be suitable for accommodating a second family.

I managed to reassure my father after explaining that I was aware of all the duties and responsibilities marriage would entail, especially after describing the progress I had made at work. He asked if I had chosen someone, to which I replied affirmatively. He then advised me to inquire about her and her family, asking me to provide him with their name and address so he could also investigate.

According to him, it was essential to gather information before committing, as the matter was very serious and would affect the rest of my life positively or negatively. Therefore, he advised me to be cautious and take my time in selecting the right person.

I told him that I had already done some inquiries and gave him **Maya**'s family name and address. I expressed my desire to get engaged in four months. Initially, he was surprised by the long timeframe, but I convinced him by explaining that it would allow enough time for inquiries and give me some financial relief.

I don't remember ever leaving a conversation with my father feeling as happy and satisfied as that time. He accepted all my ideas and agreed to my requests, which was an excellent and motivating start. From then on, I lived my beautiful dream on one hand, but under the pressure of the countdown to the awaited date on the other.

Finally, **Caleb**, **Uncle Sebastian**'s son, returned from abroad after completing his studies and obtaining his degree from a Canadian university. We organized a small welcoming party at work to celebrate the occasion. Everyone was happy and enjoying the moment. I was just as pleased, as I had always been moved by stories of family reunions after long absences.

However, I was slightly reserved, fearing losing my new position after only two months. I suspected that **Uncle Sebastian** might be planning to delegate the store's management to his son from then on. But my fears soon dissipated when he expressed his desire to keep me in my position while **Caleb** took over his father's role, allowing **Uncle Sebastian** to rest more.

I found **Caleb** to be a smart and elegant young man who cared greatly about his appearance. At first, he seemed arrogant and conceited. In the beginning, I was reserved in my interactions with him, but soon a friendly relationship developed between us, based on mutual respect.

He accompanied me throughout the working hours to learn about the work environment and understand the nature of transactions with customers. He had a strong desire to develop his father's business, constantly studying new plans and objectives to increase income. He worked on diversifying distribution sources and planning to establish local production facilities. I admired his ambitious goals, though I doubted the feasibility of achieving them, given the difficulties in our country that hinder such projects.

We began discussing his projects whenever we had free time at work. Eventually, we started talking about almost everything, from his experiences abroad to his adventures with foreign friends and even his romantic stories with girls.

Caleb noticed my frequent phone usage due to the numerous text messages I received and sent daily. He didn't keep the question to himself but instead boldly asked me at one point, with a sly smile on his face: "Do you have a girlfriend, **Mason**?"

I was surprised by his question and stuttered for a moment. It was awkward for me to talk about my romantic relationship with someone I had known for a short time, but I understood that **Caleb** had learned to speak his mind without hesitation from his time with foreigners.

I hesitated a bit before answering: "Yes, I've been in a relationship with a girl for a long time, and I want to marry her."

He then bombarded me with many questions, to which I answered cautiously, as I wasn't comfortable discussing my future life partner with someone I didn't fully trust. I was very careful in my dealings with **Caleb**, but over time and with frequent interactions, I got to know his true nature more and more. I found him to be a kind and honest person, qualities that dispelled all my doubts. Our relationship progressed smoothly, leading to a strong bond that positively impacted our work. We both had promising ideas and aspirations, discussing plans and making decisions that quickly improved the store's economic aspect and working conditions. **Uncle Sebastian** was so pleased with our progress that he started calling us the "genius duo."

He was overjoyed with our accomplishments, promising me a salary increase if I continued at the same pace. This promise felt like a dream to me, as the raise meant stability and no need to think about changing jobs. With another salary increase, I would come closer to earning what someone in my field of study would make, allowing me to plan for the future, improve my life, and achieve my goals.

Seventeen days remained until the awaited birthday, meaning the engagement date was approaching. I planned to start arranging everything right after meeting **Maya**'s father, but I needed my father's approval first. Nearly three and a half months had passed without him providing me with a response regarding his inquiries about **Maya** and her family.

I was on the bus returning from work when my phone rang; it was a call from my father. I was puzzled because it was unusual for him to call me at that time. I quickly pressed the answer button and raised the phone to my ear.

I spoke with clear concern: "Hello, Dad, how are you?"

My father replied: "I'm fine. I just wanted to discuss something regarding the engagement."

He spoke in a reassuring tone, but as soon as he mentioned the word "engagement," my anxiety grew.

"Stop, please," I asked the bus driver. I had reached my stop and almost missed it, continuing to the next one.

I replied as I was getting off the bus: "I'm coming home right now; let's talk about it..."

My father stopped me, saying: "No need for that, I'll be home late today, which is why I'm calling you now."

I stepped onto the sidewalk, sweating from the tension: "Yes, Dad, go ahead, say what you need to say..."

My father was silent for a moment, then replied: "I inquired about the girl and her family among my acquaintances. The truth is, I only heard praise and commendations about them. Therefore, I advise you to proceed and set a date for the engagement."

I was so happy to hear those words from my father that I kept smiling even after the call ended.

I said: "But there's an important request I want to make, Dad."

My father answered cautiously: "Speak, what is your request?"

I spoke, fearing rejection: "I'll make sure to reach out to the girl's father and talk to him on the phone to arrange a meeting, but I want you to be by my side when I do."

My father laughed warmly and said: "Alright, **Mason**, I'll be by your side. Make sure the meeting is scheduled for the weekend."

I exhaled lightly, feeling relieved of a heavy burden, and said: "Of course, Dad, whatever you want."

Father: "Goodbye, my son."

Me: "Goodbye, Dad."

I ended the call and immediately contacted **Maya**. It was good that I hadn't discussed the topic with her recently, which eased the pressure of anticipation and allowed me to arrange things calmly.

She answered after a few rings: "Hello."

I stopped in a quiet spot to speak more comfortably.

I said: "Hello, Snow White, how are you?"

She replied in a low voice: "I'm fine, and you?"

I smiled and said: "I couldn't be better. I have some good news. I won't keep you long; the engagement process is moving in the right direction as planned. So, I need your father's number to discuss the matter and arrange a date to coordinate everything."

She answered in an even quieter tone, as if whispering: "Okay, I can't talk now. I have to go. I'll call you later."

My smile turned to confusion and worry, and I asked: "What's wrong, **Maya**? Is there a problem?"

As I asked, I felt the phone vibrate—it was because she had hung up on me!!

I didn't know what had happened. She had never done that before. She always waited for me to finish speaking before ending the call. Something urgent must have caused her to act this way. My confusion turned to anxiety. I was about to call her back immediately, but then I remembered her saying, "I'll call you later." Perhaps it wasn't the right time to call her, so I decided to wait and anticipate her call.

At 9 PM, nearly four hours had passed, and I kept an eye on my phone every five minutes, fearing I might miss her call. I couldn't wait any longer. I checked Messenger to see if she had been online and read the message I sent right after our call.

It wasn't like her to take this long to reply. I couldn't control myself and decided to call her. The phone rang, but there was no answer, which raised my suspicions and increased my fears. I tried a second and third time but got the same result.

It was past midnight, so I decided to stay home, thinking a lot, unable to sleep. My anxiety heightened when I received a message notification. I eagerly checked it and saw it was from **Maya**. There was something wrong!

The first thing that caught my attention was that **Maya** had logged out of Messenger immediately after I logged in. The second thing was the unusually long message, which read:

"Hello **Mason**, I'm sorry for not contacting you. I'm going through some personal issues that don't allow me to do so. I've thought a lot about what you said regarding arranging a meeting with my father, and I think it's not the right time to take this step. I hope you understand the situation and stop thinking about it for now. Please don't call or text me during this period until I contact you. I need some time to sort things out in my life, so please give me some space to organize things. I ask for your understanding and consideration of the circumstances I'm going through... Goodbye."

I couldn't comprehend what she meant. I didn't even understand what she was referring to. I tried messaging her to find out what was going on, but to no avail. I didn't receive a response. More than three years had passed since our first meeting, and we had both gone through difficult times. She always shared her crises with me in great detail, asking for my help and listening to my advice. I had always supported her through her hardships. So why was she excluding me now?

Wait!!... Could I be the problem? Maybe her father found out about our relationship, and she is currently in trouble with her family because of me. That would explain her request for no contact. My heart raced with fear for my beloved. I felt a surge of urgency to talk to **Uncle Omar** to save **Maya** from this predicament, but I couldn't understand her request regarding meeting her father and her words, "Stop thinking about it."

There were too many ambiguous things causing me a headache.

It was 1:30 AM, and I was still awake, lost in thought. I didn't know what to think or do. I couldn't close my eyes or even feel tired—just a headache and a stream of thoughts replacing each other. My brain was working weakly and disheartened, searching for a logical explanation for what was happening, but it found no convincing answer.

At 3 AM, the mere thought that I needed to sleep and go to work in the morning chased away any drowsiness and fueled my mind to think more, increasing my confusion and anxiety. I decided to skip work and go to the university to meet **Maya** and uncover the unknown.

I woke up at 6:45 AM after three hours of sleep. I messaged **Caleb** to inform him of my absence, citing an urgent situation. I took a taxi to the university, knowing where I would find her. She usually took a student bus that arrived before 8 AM. So, I headed straight to the bus stop in front of the university entrance and leaned my head against a wall facing the station after getting my morning coffee.

The clock showed 7:50 AM. The awaited bus arrived after 20 minutes of waiting. I recognized it by the sign with the name of the city it came from. A large crowd was inside the vehicle. I decided to get closer to avoid missing **Maya** among the crowd. I watched every person disembarking from the bus, feeling relieved when I saw her stepping onto the sidewalk.

I approached a bit to catch her attention, but I noticed something strange!... She seemed cheerful and carefree, showing no signs of worry. She was clinging to a friend's arm and whispering in her ear, causing them both to burst into laughter. She hadn't noticed me, so I needed to get closer.

I heard her friend express mock annoyance about the crowded bus (like sardines in a can), causing them to laugh again. I made a hurried move and called her name softly.

She looked towards me, her laughter turning to astonishment. She stopped in her tracks while her friend continued a few steps ahead.

I initiated the conversation in a low voice: "Good morning, how are you?"

She glanced around nervously, as if worried about being seen together, and responded: "What are you doing here?"

I raised my eyebrows in surprise at her question and said: "What's going on? I need an explanation."

She shifted the bag she was carrying in front of her, gripping it with both hands as if seeking protection from me—a reaction that raised many doubts in my mind.

She spoke while preparing to move past me: "There's nothing major. I have an important meeting with the professor in a few minutes, and I mustn't be late."

I felt intense anxiety. My hand holding the coffee cup was visibly trembling.

She added, after taking a step forward: "I can't talk now. I have to go."

I spread my arms to stop her and said: "Then I'll wait for you. I'll be here after your meeting."

Fear appeared on her face after my suggestion, and she started to stammer: "No, I won't be able to meet you. I have a busy day with experiments and research. As you know, I'm preparing for my graduation project."

My anxiety intensified, and I raised my voice, asking more questions: "You won't move from here until I get a convincing answer. Talk now... What's happening? You must be hiding something important. Speak... What are you hiding from me? Talk, **Maya**, I know you well. Be honest, what has changed so suddenly?"

She glanced around again, this time out of embarrassment from the passersby hearing our conversation. She gestured with her hands for me to lower my voice and said: "I'm serious about the professor's meeting, so I must go now, or I'll be late. I'll talk to you later to explain everything."

I fixed my eyes on hers, scrutinizing her for a moment, then asked: "When will you call?"

She averted her gaze to the ground and said: "This evening, but please don't call me before that... I'll call... that's a promise."

I stepped aside, letting her pass. Lowering my head, I walked away, staggering without a farewell or even a reassuring glance. I wandered aimlessly for over fifteen minutes before snapping out of that period of madness.

I couldn't bear staying in that state all day. I needed to occupy myself with something to distract me from the bitterness of my situation. I found no way out but to go to work. I called **Caleb** and told him I had taken care of my urgent matter early and asked if I could come to work later. He replied that he needed me, and there was no need for formalities as we were like brothers.

Caleb's words lifted some of the gloom inside me. It's rare to find an employer who treats his employees in such a motivating and supportive way. That day was unlike any other. I couldn't bring myself to my best state despite repeated attempts to lift my spirits. Everyone was surprised by my frequent daydreaming. Many customers noticed the absence of my usual smile and the decline in service speed.

I made excuses to everyone who asked, saying I needed sleep. I finished my workday with great difficulty, but it was better than staying idle and drowning in thought, which would have frayed my nerves. As evening approached, I counted the minutes and checked my phone, eagerly awaiting **Maya**'s call.

Chapter Six

Night had fallen, and I couldn't bear sitting at home, waiting for her call. The darkness only heightened my anxiety. I went out to walk through the alleys of the old neighborhoods, seeking solace in my solitude and embracing my thoughts in silence, trying to piece together what had happened in the morning to understand what was going on.

I felt the emptiness in my stomach with my hand, but I had no energy to eat. I hadn't tasted food since my morning coffee and had no appetite. I wandered for nearly an hour, covering almost all parts of the city. I wouldn't need to trim my nails in the coming days since I had bitten them down due to the anxiety swirling around me.

It was nearing 9 PM, and she still hadn't called. I was beginning to fear she wouldn't. I couldn't wait any longer. I hesitated to call her dozens of times, holding the phone to dial her number but something stopped me, as if I had made a vow not to call her first.

A strange feeling washed over me, a mix of anxiety, sadness, and longing. I was so distracted that I couldn't remember what I had been thinking just moments ago. The vibration in my pocket made me stop walking and reach for my phone, followed by a ringtone confirming an incoming call. I quickly pulled out the phone to see the caller's name... It was the anticipated call. I pressed the answer button quickly and spoke in a tone void of warmth.

I said: "Hello."

She replied with a wavering voice, full of hesitation: "Hello..."

Silence lingered for a moment before I broke it: "Talk... I'm listening to what you have to say. Please clarify things."

She responded with an irritating, coy question: "What do you want to know?"

I suppressed my anger, trying to keep calm, and spoke sensibly: "You know very well what I want to know, but there's no harm in repeating it. I want to understand everything happening with you. What is the personal issue you're going through? Why did you say it's not the right time to meet your father? And why did you ask me to stop thinking about the engagement?"

The conversation fell silent again. This time, I didn't want to interrupt the quiet. I moved to a corner away from people and sat, listening to her breathing for several seconds.

She finally spoke, and I wished she hadn't. I wished she had stayed silent forever. Her words were like a dagger, disregarding my feelings without mercy. More than three years of affection and love should have at least stopped her from uttering those words. Her breath ceased, and she spoke, forcing me to hold mine: "I think it's time for us to part ways..."

I didn't comprehend what I had heard immediately. After a moment, I cautiously said: "What are you talking about? What separation are you referring to?"

She replied with clear, unfeeling firmness: "I'm sorry, we can't continue together. I've thought a lot about this before making my decision and found it to be the best solution."

My nerves began to boil, and I raised my voice gradually: "What solution are you talking about? You must be joking. Everything was fine just recently. How can you say you've thought a lot about it? Moreover, we haven't had any conflict or disagreement lately. I can't believe what you're saying—it's utterly illogical."

I didn't realize how serious she was until I heard her crying on the other end of the phone. Hearing that made me understand the gravity of my situation. My tongue felt tied, and I couldn't utter a word.

She spoke with a voice broken by deep breaths: "I'm sorry, **Mason**, for saying this is the end. I want you to know I won't change my mind."

I said angrily: "Why are you crying? I'm the one who should be angry. I really don't understand you. You're the one breaking up with me, not the other way around. I want to understand something: Did I do something to upset you? Did I wrong you? Did I..."

She interrupted me: "No, you didn't do anything wrong. The decision is about me."

She added: "I'm going to hang up now. Please don't try to call me, and you need to forget about me."

I quickly said: "Wait, I want to ask one question."

She firmly replied: "Did you ever love me?"

She responded immediately, without hesitation, as if she had rehearsed the answer: "I thought I did, but I discovered otherwise."

I asked again: "Is there someone else involved?"

Silence lingered for a moment, followed by the buzzing of a disconnected call... She had hung up.

I tried calling her again, but her phone was off. I tried every possible way to contact her, but all my attempts failed. I wished it was a nightmare from which I would soon wake. My strength waned, and I felt a suffocating urge to cry bitterly.

I wished I could scream to ease the pain inside me, even a little. I didn't care if I cried in the middle of the street, in front of passersby, but I couldn't bring myself to do it. Not a single tear escaped my eyes to relieve my chest. My heart was clenched, my body exhausted, and all I had left was to be rational and find solace.

I can't sleep; my mind is preoccupied... I think deeply... I repeat the same questions and my being is in amazement and wonder... Did she leave me!? Did her feelings change this quickly, or was she pretending all these years? More than three years... Really!?

After spending a sleepless night thinking and regretting without a blink of an eye, I decided to skip work and go to the university again to meet **Maya** hoping to bring her back to her senses. I went in the morning to wait for her at the bus station, but she didn't show up. I remained in the same state for three consecutive days without any sign of her. My body deteriorated due to inconsistent sleep and poor nutrition.

Maya worked on canceling all the connections between us, she blocked me on social media and either closed or changed her phone number. These are signs of her determination to distance herself from me. I must maintain what little dignity I have left and accept the situation.

However, I won't rest until I'm completely sure of her desire to separate. I didn't believe **Caleb** even after everything I heard with my own ears. All I want is to see her and ask the question once more... Did you love me? To observe her eyes at the moment of response and compare them with the look she had when she first confessed her love for me.

Today is Thursday. I decided to go to work after three days of absence. I haven't slept well recently, I have no desire to eat or talk, let alone joke around. I think it's a phase of depression, and I hope it doesn't last longer. I fear staying in this state for a long time, all I do is drift and think all day...

There is clear tension from my employers due to repeated absences without a clear reason, but neither **Caleb** nor my uncle **Sebastian** have issued any warnings or reprimands, although **Caleb** tried to find out the reason for my absence and offered help if needed.

I had a very hard day, unable to cope with the work pressure. I made a calculation error that could have led to a severe loss had it not been for the customer's honesty. This happened in front of **Caleb**. It would have been a disgrace to my career if it hadn't been caught. Even a newcomer to the job wouldn't be allowed to make such a mistake. It hurt my pride, and I couldn't swallow it despite avoiding the loss...

In the evening, while lying in my room staring into space and escaping far with my mind to ease my loneliness, I received a call from **Adrian**. I hesitated before answering... I had never hesitated to answer my best friend before... It seems my mental state prefers isolation at this stage.

I said, "Hello **Adrian**, how are you?" He replied worriedly, "How are you? I haven't seen you for days. I'm waiting for you at home, I've downloaded an exciting movie, and I'm waiting to watch it together tonight..." He added, "Oh, I almost forgot, my mom invites you to dinner. It's your lucky day; your favorite dish is almost ready."

I understood from his words that his mother prepared my favorite food, but I didn't feel like watching movies or eating. All I wanted was to be alone...

I tried to evade: "I'm very tired today. I don't think I have the energy to stay up. I'd prefer to stay home... I'm sorry, I can't come." **Adrian** expressed his surprise, saying, "Someone like you giving up such delicious food? There must be something wrong, what's the matter?" I took a deep breath and said, "I broke up with **Maya**." Then I corrected myself and said, "Rather, she left me..."

His voice changed suddenly, as if he switched from sluggishness to alertness. I bet he changed his position from lying down to sitting up. That's how he usually is; he prefers a ready position when receiving surprising news. He said, "What? You and **Maya** broke up? ... Since when?" I said regretfully, "A few days ago." **Adrian** replied in a strong tone, "A few days ago, and you didn't tell me? That explains your absence. Are you hiding such news from me?" I apologized, saying, "No, my friend. I intended to tell you, but my mental state urges me to keep quiet and isolate." **Adrian**: "I won't talk much today; you will tell me all the details. You have two options: either you come and tell me the events in my room alone, or I swear I'll come to your house, and we'll have the conversation in **Damian's** presence..."

After his oath, I had no choice but to go to his house. I started narrating all the details, and he listened attentively for over an hour. I won't lie; I felt some psychological relief after sharing my burden with another party.

Adrian spoke after intertwining his fingers and resting his chin on them: "I'll be honest with you, my friend. I know very well how attached you were to **Maya** and the extent of your sincerity and good intentions. Honestly, I expected this scenario initially and feared the consequences for you. But after the first year passed and I witnessed the harmony between you two, I dismissed those negative thoughts from my mind. I know the feeling you're going through, my friend, because I've been through a similar situation long ago. You know my story with my girlfriend during middle school and the love I had for her. Losing her caused the hardness of heart and emotional coldness that I currently live with, which you have always found strange and blamed me for.

He added: "Listen carefully to what I will say to you. I have an idea I want to share with you. It will be a secret between us. You need to prepare yourself for a very tough period. Your only mistake was loving **Maya** sincerely, and that's why you won't be able to forget her easily. You will lose months, if not years, to recover and be ready for a new relationship. So, I have a solution for you, which is the best option among all solutions. The strange irony is that the opportunity came at the right time."

I said in confusion: "Could you stop speaking in riddles? You have increased my tension. What are you talking about?" **Adrian** got up from his place and approached me, then looked into my eyes seriously and said: "Migration, my friend... Migration." I thought for a moment that he was talking to someone else, as he knows well that migration is the last thing on my mind. I shook my head, asking: "What migration are you talking about? You know well that I prefer living here in my homeland." He brought his palm close to my face and signaled no with his index finger: "No... You can't continue living here like this. You will waste a lot of time before you get yourself back. I am currently preparing to go alone, but now I must take you with me. Loneliness will destroy you; losing your loved one and after a while, I won't be here beside you. This will certainly break you..."

I said: "I'm not yet sure of **Maya's** desire to distance herself from me. I must meet her and talk to her. There is something I did not understand in her words. I fear there might be something hidden that made her ask for separation beyond her capability. So, I won't enter into this discussion with you."

I added: "I remembered, you blamed me a lot for hiding the news for days. Here you are, determined to leave alone without telling me, and it appears that you have been planning this for a long time."

Adrian replied, trying to justify: "You know very well that I have been planning to migrate for a long time. I recently found the right opportunity, so I will seize it and leave the country."

I asked, "Did you finally get the visa?" **Adrian** sighed and said after lying back down on his bed: "No, **Mason**, I didn't. I will travel through illegal immigration."

The news hit me like a calamity, adding another ordeal to my distress. We then engaged in a futile argument from which I understood that no one could dissuade **Adrian** from his decision. Furthermore, he tried once more to renew his offer for me to accompany him to Europe.

We stayed in this state until late at night without convincing each other. So, we decided to sleep and postpone the discussion to a later time. That night, I felt something strange that eased my sorrow and weakness. I felt as if I would find a way out of my situation. It seems that the conversation with **Adrian** had some benefit despite its intensity and many disagreements.

I woke up on Sunday morning, planning to go to the university to meet **Maya** and talk to her. I tried to communicate with her in various ways, but to no avail. I tried messaging one of her close friends on Messenger, but to my surprise, I found that she had blocked me just minutes after I sent my text message.

Certainly, her action was due to **Maya's** advice. I missed work again, but this time I had taken permission from my uncle **Sebastian** in advance. I dedicated the entire day to meeting her. I left the house with the firm intention not to miss her encounter this time.

What I wanted was to confirm her rejection of me. My goal was to eliminate all doubts and hear her answer while looking into her eyes. I wanted to give her the reasons so that one day I wouldn't blame myself for losing my love without inquiry and investigation. I tried to bury my pride to verify her unwillingness to continue with me and to ensure there were no hidden matters forcing her to distance herself from me.

I stayed at the university gate as I had done previously, waiting for her bus to arrive. I did not want to miss her this time. I was determined to stay in front of the entrance even if it took the whole day. After a short period, the desired vehicle arrived. I watched calmly as she got off, but it was in vain. Neither she nor her friend were on the bus. It seemed she was avoiding meeting me during this period, knowing that I would come looking for her.

I sat down again, my eyes not missing anyone passing by. I looked like someone with no purpose, whose only concern was to sit and spy on others' lives. About an hour and a half passed before I saw her approaching the place where I was sitting. It was clear she came using public transportation. She quickened her pace when she saw me, and she walked on the far side of the pavement, trying to avoid meeting me. I didn't realize how I jumped and found myself holding her hand.

I said cautiously to avoid drawing attention: "Please wait, I just want a few seconds." She replied angrily without slowing her pace: "Stay away from me, or I will scream and gather the crowds around you."

I tightened my grip on her wrist and said: "I will not leave, even if it's on my dead body. I want to ask you some questions. I have the right to know. I spent almost three and a half years of my life with you, so I deserve to clarify some things, and it won't take much of your time."

She stopped walking and turned to look at my face, and said: "I have said everything and made clear my desire in our last conversation. I meant every word I said, so leave me alone."

I said after looking deeply into her eyes: "Really? Did you mean everything? Is it true that you don't love me?"

She looked into my eyes with a harsh look as if she was taking on a challenge and spoke words that were like a stab to my heart: "Yes, I do not love you. Can you leave me now?"

My hand gradually loosened from her wrist until I let go. She turned and continued her way while I remained rooted in my place until she disappeared from my sight. That meeting hurt me to the extent that I saw darkness around me. What is happening to me? Why have I come to hate everything?

I have never loathed life before as much as I despise it now. I no longer find any taste in this world. Why all this torment? Is this what I deserve?... When I found the sweetness of life after the hell I lived through after my mother's death, I sacrificed all my effort to turn that misery into happiness.

Here I am now back to the starting point. Here is the departure of another dear person to my heart, shattering the dreams and hopes I built over the years. Maybe this is my destiny, perhaps sadness and misery are written in my fate. I wish I could go back in time to three and a half years ago.

I wouldn't have paid attention to her in the library, and if I did, I wouldn't have given her that care and attention all this time. I wouldn't have built my future and aspirations on her. With one word, everything collapsed before my eyes.

I will never forget the harshness of that look as long as my heart beats. Was she that skilled in acting all this time, or was I just a fool blinded by love? Truly, it is said that love is blind... It didn't just blind my eyes; it blinded all my senses and emotions. But I am not to be blamed to that extent; she was indeed very skilled in acting, worthy of an Oscar for her performance.

Oh, whom I named Snow White and made my own, you have shattered my heart and spirit. I don't know how to mend what you have done to me. I don't know how it will end. The future has become unknown and frightening since I planned for it with you by my side. I have lost the desire to live. I will never think of suicide, but I understand more what those who commit it go through. I suffer from severe depression, but there's nothing I can do.

Many say the only cure for those in my situation is time. I couldn't bear all this misery for a few days, so how can I endure it for the coming years? Everything reminds me of you, wherever I go and wherever I am, I find something that brings me back to past memories. The songs we shared, the gifts I received from you, the neighborhood spots where I secluded myself while talking to you on the phone, my phone... my phone where I spent all my sweet and bitter times chatting with you, in short.

Everything around me has a memory with you, and every place I escape to makes me think of you more. I have seriously started considering what **Adrian** said. Is migration the solution? Will leaving the homeland remove the distress I live in? I don't think I will ever forget **Maya**. Maybe migration will alleviate the sorrow and depression within me.

I never imagined that love could do this to me. **Maya**, you are truly my beloved, and you will remain so no matter what you have done to me. But I cannot forgive you for what you have done to me... I will not forgive you.

Chapter Seven

When evening came and I was lying in my bed messaging **Adrian**, intending to catch up and plan our evening together, I heard my father's voice calling for my immediate presence. Everyone in the house noticed I wasn't acting like myself, especially my stepmother **Vivian**, who kept asking me repeatedly about my condition. I always answered that I was fine. I was thinking a lot about what **Adrian** said about migration. My meeting with **Maya** this morning made me consider the matter more seriously, but migrating illegally and throwing myself into the perilous sea waves is something I won't accept for myself or **Adrian**.

I found my father in the kitchen. I sat across from him at the table while **Vivian** was preparing dinner.

"How are you?" my father asked, as if interrogating me without any preamble.

I replied, "I'm fine." He asked again, "Is everything okay?" I replied, "Yes, everything is fine." He asked, "How are things going regarding the engagement? You haven't told me anything new despite our conversation days ago. What did the girl's father tell you? When will we meet him?"

I was shocked by all these questions. It was difficult to answer them individually, let alone all at once.

I shook my head and replied, "No, father, we won't meet him. I haven't even spoken to him."

He looked at me with a puzzled expression and asked, "What delayed you like this? Is there something wrong?" I replied without realizing where I came up with that answer, "Apparently, I was late; the girl is engaged to someone else."

My father spoke in confusion, "Are you sure?... I asked one of my acquaintances who is close to their neighbors, and he didn't tell me what you're saying."

His words injected me with a dose of fear; I was terrified of him discovering my lie. I wasn't used to lying to my father, but I couldn't face him with the truth.

I replied, "Yes, she has been engaged for not that long." **Vivian** turned around after covering the pot on the stove and started speaking to me, "Why did you keep such news to yourself? I would have initiated preparations for the engagement. You should have told us..."

I turned to her and said, "Sorry, **Vivian**, I only found out recently. I was about to inform all of you, but I didn't find the right time."

At that point, my father said, "No worries, son. Marriage is a matter of fate. Look for another girl, and I will always be here to help you."

Vivian stepped closer and said, "We will help you find the right girl if you don't mind."

I said, "No, I won't start searching immediately. I think I rushed a bit. I'll wait a while to prepare myself more, and I'll let you know when I need a helping hand."

After dinner, I asked my father for permission to go to **Adrian**, who was eagerly waiting for my arrival, especially after I informed him in a text message about what happened to me in the morning. All he wants now is for us to leave together for Europe. We both know that tonight's conversation is crucial and might result in one of us being convinced by the other's opinion.

I sat in front of **Adrian** after greeting him, and I went straight to the point, asking him to tell me all the details of his plan.

I know very well that he is a smart person and doesn't make such decisions without taking the necessary precautions, so I decided to listen to all his statements before trying to convince him to stay since he is the only one living with his elderly parents. He seemed pleased after I decided to listen to his plan, which he believed would convince me. He sat cross-legged on his bed after putting the TV on mute and started saying, "Please don't interrupt me."

I nodded in agreement without saying a word. Then he began to outline his plan, saying, "I previously told you about an Italian girl named **Elisa**, a nice 20-year-old girl I have been in contact with for about two years. But recently, over the past six months, a special emotional relationship developed between us, to the point that **Elisa** asked me to come and live in Italy. I expressed my desire to be with her, and she agreed. That happened two months ago. I didn't want to tell you at the time for fear of your criticism and rebuke.

I started planning to go to Italy after losing hope of getting a visa. Some time ago, I got to know a person named **Henry** who works in a secret network in the eastern part of the country, organizing illegal migration operations. I used to talk to him usually to inquire about some details related to migration in general. Over time, we became friends and started talking on the phone now and then, and most of the time, we communicated via the internet.

I asked him to inquire about a trip to Italy with the intention of going on it. He refused to talk on the phone and asked me to come to a safe place. We agreed to meet on Tuesday, the day after tomorrow, to answer my questions. If I am convinced, we might agree on the remaining arrangements and the travel date. As for you, I talked to **Elisa** a lot about you, and she has known you for a long time.

I recently told her about the difficult circumstances you are going through that prevent you from living a normal life and informed her about the possibility of you accompanying me. I also asked her to look for a modest apartment that we both could share until my wedding preparations are done. Her response was that there was no problem with that as long as you are my best friend, and she added that she would welcome us warmly, which is a source of her joy. She also expressed her happiness at having a close person who would be like my family in a foreign country. As for **Henry**, I talked to him about a friend of mine being interested in the trip, and his request was for you to come with me on Tuesday.

We will go to Italy together and share the same house, maybe even the same job. We will find you a girl who suits you, and you will also get married, so both of us will stay there with a legal residence. What do you think about all this?"

I sat stunned by the calamity of what I heard. I was amazed by every word he said.

I began to express what was on my mind: "So everything is related to a foreign girl you befriended online. Look at my situation and learn from my experience. Years of dating led to nothing but mirages. How can you trust a girl after all this?"

I never heard such foolish talk from you all these years I've known you. What marriage are you talking about? What shared house? Everything hinges on whether the girl is trustworthy. Besides, it's not in my nature to take such risks.

Everything you've said is built on a flimsy foundation. You could marry the Italian girl in safer ways without taking risks. Stop being reckless, **Adrian**. You can marry her and then go after completing all the preparations and paperwork. Also, I smell a marriage of convenience brewing on your strings, and typically such marriages don't last long and result in conflicts between the parties, which inevitably lead to separation. It seems you've lost your mind, **Adrian**.

Adrian responded with his face turning red from anger: "Why such pessimism? I'm not a little kid. I know very well what I'm about to do. It might seem silly to you, but I spent a lot of time to come up with a similar solution. This solution is the result of a great effort I made. As for the marriage of convenience you claim, I will prove my love and loyalty to **Elisa** at the right time. I have known many foreign girls before, and what I can say now is that **Elisa** is incomparable to any other girl. We are currently living an exceptional love story, and I won't let any circumstance stop me from completing it by getting married.

Preparing the files and paperwork might seem easy to you, but let me remind you that we live in a bureaucratic environment, and the ways of formalizing a relationship you're talking about may take months, if not years. I can't wait that long…"

We argued all night until we reached a temporary solution that satisfied both parties. The decision will be made after meeting **Henry** and experiencing it together. Each of us knows the other's goal from the trip. While he will try to gradually convince me, I intend to search and investigate all the negative aspects to find excuses to make him back out, in addition to my discomfort with him going alone to a new place among strangers.

Each of us went to bed to sleep. One question occupied my mind: How will I ask for a two-day leave from work? My God, how hard life is. Overnight, my life took a turn to experience something I didn't choose. Everything I planned went down the drain. I have to live my fate as it is destined. There are things we encounter in our lives that we have to face without our will.

I requested a week off, which was the best solution to avoid repeated absences from work. **Caleb** initially showed some surprise but approved the idea after I pointed out the disruption and loss of focus that afflicted me in the past days. I justified it by not getting enough rest since I started the job, which affected my psyche and took away my discipline recently.

Adrian and I agreed to wake up the next day at four in the morning to catch the trip to the east of the country, which was scheduled at five to five. The distance between my city and the meeting place is about six hundred kilometers, meaning a journey of at least ten hours by bus.

We prepared that night for the trip and informed our families that it was just a normal tour for relaxation and exploration. We finally arrived at the required place after about twelve hours of exhausting travel. **Henry** welcomed us warmly, contrary to my expectations. I found him to be a kind and calm-looking person.

I expected to meet a man resembling the cunning characters we are used to seeing in thief and gangster movies. Before arriving, my heart was gripped with anxiety and suspicion, but with the first contact with **Henry**, I found that my psyche relaxed significantly.

He invited us to sit with him in one of the cafes before asking us where we planned to spend our night. **Adrian** didn't finish his answer about us intending to stay in one of the hotels when he swore, we would sleep at his house and have dinner with him.

I was really surprised by his generosity and hospitality and started questioning myself: Is he that close to **Adrian**, or are these just tricks to gain our trust?

We sat on the rooftop of the house under the bright starlight, sipping tea after dinner. **Henry** didn't appear to be wealthy, on the contrary, he seemed to be of modest means. Despite that, he hosted and welcomed us exceedingly well. I was surprised that the discussion about migration hadn't yet come up.

Since our arrival, most of our conversation revolved around the hardships of travel and introducing the area and its customs. Everything indicated that we were on a sightseeing tour as we had told our families. But after a short while, I decided to bring up the topic and took the initiative to speak. While **Henry** was narrating stories about the difficult living conditions in the area, I seized the opportunity to talk.

I said after placing my tea on the table, "Excuse me, **Henry**, but does this have anything to do with many of the area's residents organizing illegal migration?"

Henry replied, "Yes, of course, **Mason**. Unfortunately, many of my acquaintances make a living from it. There are many merchants of sailing supplies. Some make and repair boats, and some specialize in fixing engines. There are also those who navigate the migrant boats to the other shore. There are others like me who gather migrants and organize the trips. All of this is done in complete secrecy."

His answer piqued my curiosity, and I asked again: "What do you gain from such a risky endeavor?"

Adrian showed his disapproval of my question with a look that I understood as wanting to scold me, but **Henry** didn't seem annoyed by the question and answered openly: "It's my job, which I make a living from, just like most of those who participate with us. It's risky, but we had no other choice due to the lack of suitable means to secure a livelihood. We don't have many options, which makes many of the area's youth consider undertaking the migration journey to set goals for their lost lives and achieve the dream of living a decent life despite the journey's risks and the hardship of living on the other side before settling, if they can settle, of course. But it is worth trying as long as there are possibilities in favor of achieving the goal."

I said, "I see you're not sugar-coating life in Europe, even though you organize the trips!"

He laughed and replied sarcastically: "I won't hide the truth as everything is apparent. Surely, you're a smart person and know well what you're about to do. You can do a simple search on the internet and learn many harsh realities, but don't worry. Your friend, as it seems, has planned well."

I asked once more, "Why are you staying here and not migrating?"

He replied more seriously this time: "I traveled three times to Italy through illegal migration and was the leader of the trip the last two times, but I wanted to return each time."

I asked in response to **Henry**'s statement: "Did you plan this every time? I traveled the first time as an assistant to a professional leader to learn the route and its intricacies... Since you have a lot of questions, I'll ease your burden of asking more. I will tell you some secret things because you are a friend of **Adrian**. The boat leader must be knowledgeable about the sea's intricacies because all responsibility will fall on him after setting sail."

Therefore, he must pay attention to every little detail to ensure the success of the journey. Any small mistake could put his life and the lives of the passengers at risk. Upon arriving in Europe, the boat and equipment are allowed to be used, which means the trip leader will not return and will be a migrant like the rest. The practice here is that the trip for the leader is free, in addition to receiving a salary equivalent to what a single passenger pays.

If the trip is completed safely and securely, the trip leader will be treated specially overseas due to existing connections and recommendations on his behalf. Personally, when I was in Europe, I worked for a period of time each time and made satisfactory profits, then I sent my money with one of the neighborhood boys who works on one of the commercial ships. Afterwards, I surrendered myself to the Italian authorities to be returned to my homeland.

I spoke after feeling puzzled and astonished: "Do you mean that you chose to return? It sounds like a story from one of the movies." I added, "I don't want to bother you more, but I have one last question: How do you manage to survive each time, knowing that many people die at sea?"

Henry responded: "No problem, I will answer with pleasure. All it takes is not to be reckless and to be careful, especially regarding the equipment, and not to rush in making the decision to go out to sea. The decision requires prudence and waiting for calm weather suitable for such a trip. Attention must be paid to the quality of the tools, and it is not recommended to use old and low-quality equipment as it is the weapon you will face the anger of the sea with.

I have heard of many trips that failed due to recklessness and poor equipment. However, there are still those who repeat the attempt and risk lives to save some extra money. What I can tell you is that taking the necessary precautions and measures, you will find a chance to face even the greatest difficulties and arrive safely."

Adrian spoke this time after being silent throughout the conversation: "We want to know about the upcoming trip you told me about."

Henry replied: "Of course, I will tell you all the details. First, I assure you that among those who will lead the trip is a friend of mine, an experienced fisherman. In addition, he has traveled to Italy four times as a leader. There are three boats that will depart on the same trip, and I will ensure that you are with my friend if you decide to migrate because he is the best of the three leaders. Tomorrow morning, we will go to show you the beach from which the journey will start. But before that, you must know what to provide. The first condition is to provide the trip money, which includes all expenses such as the boat, engine, GPS device, fuel, etc.

Additionally, you need to bring food for the trip, and I advise you to bring date paste and canned food because it satisfies hunger and lasts the entire fifteen-hour journey, provided everything goes well.

Another piece of advice as a brother that may help you upon arrival is to bring plastic bags with you and put your belongings, documents, and educational qualifications inside them, as well as new clothes. Then seal the bags tightly so that no water gets inside. After arrival, your clothes will get wet, so you will need to change them.

I advise you to bring a respectable amount of hard currency to last the first few days without hunger and to enable you to buy a house to shelter you. As for the money, it is best to send it through the bank to a trusted friend who will return it to you upon arrival.

Regarding the conditions, it turned out that they are available for both of us. Usually, providing the trip money is the most difficult challenge for illegal immigrants. The amount was equivalent to about three months of work in the fabric shop.

The information provided by **Henry** made me think about the matter more seriously, especially after thinking about **Adrian's** words about forgetting what happened to me recently. My involvement in this plan made me forget the torment I was going through and think about something else. What if I change my life course?

The morning arrived, and before sunrise, we left the house to take a look at the beach from which the trip would start. I started imagining how it would be in this solemn atmosphere, the calmness broken by the sound of the waves, a scene that instills fear in the heart. How many bodies have you devoured, O sea? How many exhausted bodies fought your waves, hoping for a second chance, even if it meant returning to the old miserable life? You are treacherous and cannot be trusted, but despite this, the youth of my country risk crossing you to escape the oppression caused by a failed system that cares only for its own interests.

Before taking the road back home, **Henry** informed us that the trip would take place soon because the places are limited and almost running out. He gave us two days to respond to him to finalize the reservation or the seats would be provided to other people. **Henry's** demeanor confused me; he appeared calm, as if he knew what he was doing. His words were reassuring, but is it just talk to exploit us?

I reached home in the evening, exhausted from the trip. I decided to take a short nap to regain some energy, and I wish I hadn't slept those minutes. At four in the morning, I couldn't close my eyes. Thoughts kept me awake as I tried to convince myself to stay in the homeland. The reality of migration seemed like the perfect escape, and the idea started to appeal to me. After analyzing and evaluating, I began to find the correctness and wisdom in **Adrian's** words and concepts. But from another perspective, how can I throw myself into the sea, risking my life?

Even if I refuse to take the risk, I cannot let my dearest friend risk his life alone in such an adventure. There are many disturbances, but I must make a decision as soon as possible, and all my fears boil down to regret on a day when regret will be of no use.

Easing the immense pressure, I feel in this adventure, or rather replacing an unbearable pressure with another unknown one that I still don't know if I can bear, as everything hinges on unknown consequences.

I will not forgive myself if something happens to **Adrian**. If that happens, how can I face his parents while knowing all about their son's plans without being able to stop him? I won't even be able to look at my uncle **Gabriel** and aunt **Grace**. I would rather die with **Adrian** at the bottom of the sea than live such a moment.

Adrian left me in great confusion, trying hard to get me to agree to migrate together. His words deeply affected me, saying it was our only chance to keep our friendship as it is now. He tried every way to convince me, even threatening to go no matter the cost, as if saying, "You are faced with reality, and the decision is yours because I have already made mine, and there is no turning back." His words summarized a lot, making me really confront the truth.

I know **Adrian** very well. If he decides to do something, he will undoubtedly do it. After a mental exhaustion, I finally came out of a difficult situation with a decision I made with myself. I decided to undertake the promised migration experience. I picked up my phone and wrote a text message to **Adrian** to inform him of my decision. I wanted him to wake up to news that would make him happy.

Chapter Eight

At nine in the morning, I was in a deep sleep due to staying up very late last night. The phone rang... Oh my God, I forgot to set it to silent mode. Who would call me at this time while I am on vacation? I stretched my hand, searching for the phone, following the sound without opening my eyes. I grabbed it after feeling its location with my fingers and brought it close to my face, opening one eye halfway to recognize the caller. It's **Adrian**... He must have read my message.

I answered in a low voice: "Hello."

Adrian spoke with a tone that conveyed great happiness: "Good morning, Mason. I am happy to receive your message. I apologize for calling at this time. Given the time you messaged me, you must be asleep now, but forgive me, I couldn't contain myself any longer. I am very happy to hear this news... Hello, are you with me?"

I replied: "Yes, I am listening."

Adrian continued: "I want to inform you of something important. I contacted **Henry** a short while ago and asked him to reserve places for us on the next trip. His response was positive, and he promised to fulfill the request. He also informed me that the trip is scheduled to take place in about two weeks from today."

His last words were like a slap that woke me up from my sleep. I sat up after lying down and shouted: "What have you done? Why are you in such a hurry? Have you gone mad? Shouldn't you have discussed it with me first?"

Adrian replied: "What's the point of delaying, my friend? We have made our decision. We don't have enough time for consultation. The decision is already made, so discussing it is just a waste of time. We need to prepare everything from now to avoid mistakes during the last hours before the trip."

Once again, I found **Adrian's** words convincing. Just two weeks; the time will pass quickly. I was expecting a longer duration. These might be the last days I spend in my homeland and with my family. They might even be the last days of my life.

We arrived at the specified location a few nights before the sailing date, which was not yet determined. We left behind our past and our families, telling them it was a second exploratory trip but this time it would last longer. I won't forget my brother **Damien's** puzzled look when I told him of my intention the night before leaving home. I didn't bid him a proper farewell; I couldn't bear a heartfelt goodbye. I just patted his shoulder and asked him to take care of himself and the family. He couldn't say much after confirming that the matter was settled.

When we departed, we went to one of the small hotels in a city near the port. The trip date was not yet determined, as the date depended on several factors, including evading maritime border patrols and monitoring weather and sea conditions. We remained in that state for three days before the trip was suddenly scheduled when **Henry** called at eleven-thirty at night to inform us that the departure would be in a few hours. We quickly left the hotel and headed towards the designated beach.

We were asked to stay hidden until we were given permission to appear. We hid behind rocks and trees, forming scattered groups, waiting for the signal to depart. After hours of sitting, **Henry** finally arrived and sat in the middle of our group. He asked us to follow the instructions and go directly to the largest boat upon receiving the signal, given that there were three boats for the trip. He informed us that the large boat had good engines and a functioning direction indicator, unlike one of the smaller boats, which had a poor direction indicator. Their hope was to follow our steps and movements. He added that we were in safe hands with the trip leader, **Elias**, whom he had previously told us about, and wished us luck in our journey. Then he left after bidding us farewell.

It was around two in the morning when a person waved a flashlight from the beach and faintly shouted, "Come... come." I don't remember experiencing a similar amount of fear and panic. Everyone was frozen in place. Who could take the initiative and go to board those death boats? I watched the pale faces staring at each other. Seconds of waiting felt like hours before the first immigrant moved towards the beach, seemingly volunteering for doom.

I sat next to **Adrian** inside the boat after we pushed it into the water with a group of young men under the guidance of the trip leader. Fortunately, we were experiencing a warm night, so my lower half was wet with water. I couldn't believe what was happening... I felt like I was dreaming due to the rapid events. I didn't realize we had passed the point of reconsideration until I heard the engine start.

One of the young men who later told us he was experiencing this for the second time noticed that we were leading the convoy. After asking, **Elias** informed us that we were on the best-equipped boat, giving us the advantage of leading the trip without relying on the other boats. Only then did I realize the accuracy of **Henry's** words.

The darkness was pitch-black, and we couldn't see each other well. But I could distinguish a family on the opposite side, especially after hearing the crying of children. There was a couple with their two children, a son aged eight and a daughter aged five. Their father wanted to build a new life abroad and provide an opportunity for his children to live a dignified life. A dream that drove him and his wife to risk everything they owned to achieve freedom, as the father said. The children were clearly scared, which made the young men in the group create a cheerful atmosphere to ease the pressure. It later became clear that there were two brothers among us, one of whom was suffering from a serious illness that required treatment abroad. Since the measures to go to Germany were refused, the family had to smuggle the sick person to receive treatment as soon as possible, otherwise, it would be too late.

The rest were young men aged between seventeen and thirty-two. As we approached leaving our maritime territory, the morale increased. From time to time, you could hear laughter and encouraging words. We started greeting each other as if we had known each other for a long time.

Elias asked us to avoid turning on the lights until we were a safe distance from the shore to avoid drawing the attention of the border guards. The number of passengers was seventeen, including **Elias**, all from the eastern part of the country except for three young men from the south, and **Adrian** and I from the center. As for the other boats, there were ten people on the first boat and twelve passengers on the second boat, meaning the total trip count was thirty-nine.

The other two boats were following us by the sound of our engine due to the thick darkness of the night. After about three hours of sailing, as the sky lit up...

It became clear to us that we had lost one of the boats. **Elias** decided to stop to inquire from the members of the second boat. After inquiry, they said they did not know their location and that the last time they saw them was twenty minutes ago.

The trip leaders decided to stop the engines and wait for the third boat for a while. The likely scenario is that they stopped due to a malfunction and might catch up with the convoy. Some tried to make calls to their acquaintances in the boat, but to no avail, there was no signal.

Half an hour passed, and there was no sign of them. Fear reemerged in the hearts of everyone after everyone was trying to hide their panic. After some time, **Elias** decided to continue the journey without looking back, suggesting the possibility that they were captured by the coast guards if they stopped. We all hoped for that instead of them remaining and perishing at sea.

What is on my mind now is the image of my family. Fear grips me at the thought of not gaining my father's approval due to my decision to undertake this experience without his knowledge. I look at the sky and imagine my mother's face with a smile on her lips.

A hot tear rolls down my cheek. It's good that I wiped it away quickly before any of the passengers noticed. Damn... it seems the little girl noticed my crying, her look towards me indicates pity. I ask myself in confusion... What am I doing here now? How did I get to this point?

The answer is clear... It's because of you, **Maya**. What you did to me is what drove me to do all this. It reminds me of the day we sat down for lunch as usual under the giant walnut tree in the middle of the university, where you always preferred to eat. After I started eating my piece of pizza, you immediately held my hand to stop me from eating.

I looked at your face in surprise: "What's wrong, my dear?"

You gave me that evil look that indicated a test was coming: "Since I am your dear, I want to know how much you cherish me. I have a request that I hope you will fulfill."

I did not understand what you were aiming for. All I feared at that moment was that you would ask me to share my pizza when I was starving. I told you to go ahead with your request.

You said with a smile: "I want you to be a wolf, Mason."

My confusion increased as your smile turned into a sweet laugh, and you added: "Alright, I'll explain what I mean. I read yesterday about the loyalty of a wolf to its mate. It only mates once in its life and remains loyal to its wolf for that entire time."

I replied: "Oh, I see what you're getting at. You want me to promise you loyalty and fidelity and not even think about a second wife. Isn't it too early for this? We have to get married first, but I won't argue with you on this matter. You have my promise."

Your response was unexpected, especially after you made a childish face: "You are wrong, sir. The matter of a second wife is settled in advance. I won't even allow you to think about it. No other woman will share you with me as long as I breathe. I am talking about your marriage in case I die and leave you behind. Just thinking about it gives me the urge to tear you apart."

I couldn't help but laugh then, and every time I calmed down a bit, I would look at you to see that childish face again and enter another fit of hysterical laughter.

Do you remember what my response was then? I said to you: "Of course, Snow White, I won't do that. You are my only wolf. Maybe it seemed like a joke at that moment, even my response was simple and unremarkable. But I meant every word I said. You are the only one who resides in my small heart, so I now declare to you in a message that will not reach you that there was no need for such a will because I cannot carry out anything except what you asked without you asking."

I look at my miserable state as I gamble with my life due to the fire in my chest that you ignited. I say to myself with disappointment shaking me: "Look at yourself, you are pathetic because you don't even have the ability to hate her."

Thirteen hours of continuous sailing with nothing around you but water. The sun is at its peak, announcing the time of the afternoon. Everyone is anxiously anticipating the outcome of the journey. Each one of us is sitting on plastic containers with a capacity of forty liters. There are at least twenty containers on the boat, all filled with gasoline. Looking at them makes you feel like your life is down to just moments due to the repeated warnings from **Elias**. Every time we moved forward, he asked for a new container to use for fueling the engine.

Elias recommended handling the containers with care or, as he preferred to call them, bombs. He kept saying that they could cause our demise if we didn't follow the necessary precautions, the most important of which was to avoid smoking at all costs, or else our fate would be inevitable death, as happened previously with one of the trips, resulting in the death of eight people.

Conversations were happening here and there as if we were one family facing the same fate. You could feel from their talks their desire to convince themselves that everything was alright, while the boys were adding a fun atmosphere after becoming the stars of the journey.

Elias stopped the engine and signaled the second boat to stop and approach. It seemed he was going to announce important news. He stood up before inviting us to listen, then started talking: "I inform you that we are fine and everything is going as it should. We are now on the right track and approaching a nearby island. We have about three hours left to arrive. However, we must avoid the Italian coast guard, which usually patrols along their border strip. Therefore, I suggest we wait here for a while and then set off again just before sunset to take advantage of the darkness of the night to hide.

Our destination is a beach adjacent to the port city of Porto Pino, which is near a vast forest. The island is about two hundred kilometers away from our landing spot. Upon arrival, it is preferable to disperse into small groups or even individuals, if possible, to avoid noise and evade the authorities.

If any of you are pursued by the police, I suggest you flee and hide well in the forest for a long time.

As for families and young people under the age of eighteen, there is no need to hide, as the Italian government will take the best care of you.

We chose this day to coincide with an important football match where the Italian team faces its Dutch counterpart around nine o'clock at night. Additionally, it's the weekend, tomorrow will be Sunday, and most people will be busy staying up late and celebrating, especially if their national team wins. For now, let me wish everyone good luck.

We wait in the middle of the sea in complete silence. Luckily, it is calm today. I rubbed my hands out of anxiety and fear, my attention caught by the ring on my finger. It was the ring that **Maya** had given me. I don't know why I still cling to it. Maybe I'm not ready to let go of past memories. Keeping it will always bring me back to those beautiful days. I decided to start a new chapter and focus on what lies ahead in the future.

I mustered up courage and gently removed the ring while **Adrian** watched me in silence. I held it in my hand and threw it to the farthest point in the sea, hoping to drown all the memories with the ring that is dear to me.

After hours of waiting and as the sun set, we set off again towards the desired shore using the GPS device. After a short sail and with the onset of darkness, we managed to see the lights coming from the island. A series of congratulations and hugs began among the passengers.

Happiness filled every inch of the boat. Joy seemed premature, but it was not as it appeared. It was not the result of reaching the other side of the Mediterranean, but rather a celebration of staying alive and feeling reborn after the possibility of encountering death in multiple situations.

We approached the land, feeling a noticeable drop in temperature. There was not much left to reach, and there was no sign of coast guards.

Complete silence and surveillance from the passengers. **Adrian** and I agreed to proceed directly and hide among the forest brush adjacent to the shore even if we were not chased. Upon approaching the coast, **Elias**, who showed great prowess in navigation, turned off the engine to avoid making noise and left us with the task of paddling with the boards on the deck of the boat. Meanwhile, some reckless young men started jumping with the intention of reaching the shore by swimming despite **Elias's** warning of fatigue and illness due to exposure to cold water.

They ignored his remarks. We approached cautiously and fearfully, watching some companions come ashore, visibly exhausted. Some fell on the sand, while others continued to struggle in the water.

Before jumping off the boat, **Elias** spoke, saying, "I want to point out something important that I forgot to mention earlier. There is a café called 'Mariana' owned by someone affiliated with us. It is located a few kilometers away from Porto Pino beach. You will find help there."

After helping to unload the children from the boat, **Adrian** and I started running into the unknown in the pitch darkness. We had basic information that the port was on the left, and immediately afterward, the desired forest would be there. We recognized it by its vastness as we spotted it from the sea. We identified it through the large dark part of the land and relying on that, we set off looking for those dense jungles.

We climbed a high fence and found ourselves amid dense trees and tall plants that helped to hide us. It seems that we reached the desired location after two hours of continuous running. Despite the drop in temperature and my lower half being soaked by sea water, I still didn't feel cold.

We hurried to hide among the tall grasses near one of the lakes and removed the waterproof plastic bags that we had previously secured with tape on the upper part of our bodies. The bags contained our new clothes and all the money we had converted into euros.

After sitting and waiting for a while, my body gave in to fatigue. A cold started creeping into my body, and the sounds of dogs could be heard from a distance from time to time. I hadn't slept for more than forty hours. A dreadful silence in the surroundings and no presence of animals here, a calmness that brings reassurance.

The sounds of dogs approached our location, tracking our steps. I lifted my head suddenly to take a look and found an ugly dog's face confronting me. I quickly ran behind **Adrian** who was a few meters ahead of me. The distance between us continued to increase until he disappeared from my sight. I couldn't run smoothly while the dog got closer and closer.

A group of policemen was running behind the dog to arrest me. I suddenly found myself trapped in a dead-end alley, a street with no exit, resembling a neighborhood from a famous Italian series.

The rabid dog jumped at me and grabbed my arm with its jaws, then knocked me on my back. I heard **Adrian**'s voice saying, "Mason, Mason... Wake up Mason, it's just a bad dream," as he held my wrist.

I thanked fate that it was just a nightmare. **Adrian** later told me that I had been babbling unusually. I felt my limbs which had scratches I hadn't noticed before, and a comforting feeling resulted from one of my feet being touched by sunlight. I sat in joy, realizing that dawn had arrived.

I spoke, "The sun has risen, **Adrian**. We succeeded in escaping from the police on our first night in Italy."

But **Adrian** was absorbed and paid no attention to what I said, watching behind the grasses as if waiting for something.

I looked through one of the gaps to see what was preoccupying him and saw some young men doing exercises tens of meters away. Something strange was happening; everything seemed organized and well-arranged, with walkways and benches!

Adrian suddenly spoke: "Hurry up, **Mason**, we need to get out of here. We will wear our new clothes to blend in with the people. We are in a park, not a forest."

After proceeding among the public, a sign caught our attention, showing a map of the city. We realized that we had spent the previous night in a well-known public park in the area, a park surrounded by walls on all sides. Its gates are closed at night and opened early in the morning.

It's fortunate that **Adrian** speaks Italian fluently, which made it easier for us to navigate and reach the "Mariana" café, where we received guidance and help from an elderly man to obtain mobile phone cards in order to contact our families and inform them of our arrival on Italian soil.

I quickly sent a voice message informing my brother **Damian** of our arrival while **Adrian** called his mother. I witnessed at that time the call that made my dear friend cry bitterly. Afterward, we asked the man about the safest way to leave the island towards **Catania**, which is more than seven hundred and fifty kilometers away from our current location.

The man realized that we were new immigrants and directed us to a young man named **Mark** and told us that he could help us. After a conversation with **Mark**, it became clear that some passengers from last night's trip were arrested by the Italian coast guard and gathered in a center for illegal immigrants. As for the passengers of the third boat, they were arrested by the navy due to their loss after the engine broke down near the shores. It appears that **Mark** is well-informed about all the news. Later, we found out that he is one of **Elias's** acquaintances.

Elias informed us that he had escaped police pursuit and is currently in a nearby city with a friend. The young man asked us to be patient for a few days until the security situation calms down, and then we would proceed with the trip to **Catania**. He directed us to a place where we could stay for a considerable sum of money.

After **Adrian** called **Elisa**, it became clear that **Mark** was just a scammer wanting to take advantage of our money. **Elisa** said that as long as we paid for travel tickets, there was no fear of the police. Despite this, we decided to spend that night in **Porto Pino**, knowing in advance that we were being deceived.

But there was no alternative, as all we wanted now was to spend a comfortable night after the fatigue we had endured. We decided to leave early in the morning towards the city of **Armando**, located in the **Catania** province where **Elisa** lives with her family.

According to the information **Adrian** has, the current Italian law is very lenient with foreigners; if a person is caught without documents, they will not be deported directly to their home country unless they find a document proving that they are an illegal immigrant.

This is in addition to the existence of state specialists who have innovative methods to identify the original nationality of residents. On the other hand, the state imposed strict penalties on anyone employing illegal residents, which has created a severe crisis in obtaining a job, leading many illegal travelers to resort to theft in the largest Italian cities. This has created a bad reputation among the Italian people. For this reason, **Adrian**'s plan from the beginning was to stay away from the big cities and go and live in a quiet town.

Chapter Nine

We set off early in the morning towards our destination after spending a night that felt like we were in a coma. **Armando** is known for its picturesque nature; according to **Adrian**, it is an ancient city with a rural character, containing a small population, making it quiet and free from crowds. It is located in the **Catania** province in southern Italy, in the center of the island of Sicily.

It seems we are fortunate to have reached this stage of the adventure. I had prepared myself to live through much worse, but overall, everything is going well. This means that the time we spent planning this trip was not wasted. We have the advantage of **Adrian**'s fluency in Italian, which helped divert the local people's attention from us. I knew he spoke Italian fluently, but what amazed me was that even the Italians themselves did not realize he was a foreigner due to his command of the dialect.

We need to traverse hundreds of kilometers, with part of the journey requiring sea travel. Crossing this distance is challenging, especially for strangers without any documents. We are currently traveling along roads and between cities. I comfort myself by contemplating the scenic views that bring peace to the soul. I think about my uncertain future, my family, and you, **Maya**. It is not yet time to forget you. The wound is deeper than to be healed in a short period, although what occupies my mind now is enough to distract me from the biggest worries left at home. I always wished to travel with you on our first trip abroad. How I wish you were by my side now; it would allow me to enjoy the moments I am living to forget all the hardships.

Memories of that chat more than a year ago on a hot summer night come to mind. It was after a day of relaxation I spent at the beach with my friends...

Maya: "It seems you had a great day without me while I was battling the heat at home all day."

Mason: "Today was truly enjoyable, but I prefer battling the heat beside you over going to the beach."

Maya: "I'm not sure about that. You only say this to ease my annoyance."

Mason: "Oh... you're angry then, and what has angered my Snow White?"

Maya: "You left me to suffer in loneliness all day."

Mason: "I'm sorry for my neglect. I didn't mean to, but I'll be with you starting this hour to make up for your loneliness."

Maya: "No, this alone is not enough. It won't make up for the time I spent alone."

Mason: "Enough pampering, what can I do to erase this day from your mind?"

It was clear that you were looking for a way to express something you wanted, as I had become accustomed to your childish manner when you wanted to coax me into saying something.

Maya: "You should ask me about my dreams first."

Mason: "And what are my rose's dreams?"

Maya: "I dream of traveling to Europe with my husband someday. This will allow my memory to erase the day's suffering."

Mason: "Haha, I understand what you're hinting at. I long to do that with you."

Since that day, we dreamed of a tour visiting many European landmarks. The enchanting city of Venice, located in Italy, was one of those landmarks. I never expected to visit this country without you. You were always the partner in my imagination, but fate willed otherwise.

How the soul longs for you. If you were by my side now, I would be the happiest person on earth. But your decision to leave me prevented me from living a dream you planted and ingrained in my mind.

Seven months in **Adreno** have passed like seven years. A period in which I did not find my goal at all. All I do is search for an honest livelihood enough to cover the expenses of food and rent.

We suffer daily from employers exploiting the opportunity with illegal residents by giving them low wages. We have no other choice but to accept the offers presented. If you object to it, you risk being reported to the authorities.

Adrian works as a vendor in the market at one of the greengrocers after a recommendation from **Elisa**, while I was destined to work as a porter once again. It seems that fate has destined me to work in carrying goods wherever I go. We work together in the same market, but my work is less valuable and lower-paid.

I don't have a fixed salary; every day has its earnings. The nature of my work depends on unloading goods from trucks coming from wholesale markets. I suffer from strong competition with immigrants as most of them work only to stave off hunger. This created fierce competition and led to a significant decrease in wages. The best thing I achieved during this period was the noticeable improvement I reached in the Italian language due to my interaction with people in the market.

Elisa is characterized by kindness and good treatment. She has been serving and supporting us since we arrived in **Armando**. She was the reason we found a decent house for rent at a reasonable price and is still trying to help us find respectable work for **Adrian** and me. When you see **Adrian** and **Elisa** together, everything seems to be going perfectly.

But the reality is different. The relationship is going through a severe crisis due to the absolute rejection by **Elisa**'s family of their daughter's marriage to someone residing illegally.

Especially **Elisa**'s father, who threatened to notify the authorities if he did not stay away from his daughter. He expressed his extreme opposition to immigrants many times through racial and ethnic slurs. I couldn't tolerate that every time if it weren't for thinking about my friend's best interest. It was the constant motivator that prevented me from slapping that arrogant man. Usually, **Elisa** comes to apologize and asks **Adrian** to be patient with her father's harassment.

She portrays him as having a good heart and tries to prove that he will understand the situation soon. She asks him to be patient and reassures him by reminding him of her great love for him. I always ask myself, where do I fit into all of this? While **Adrian** has a goal he is trying to stick to, what forces me to endure a similar life? How will things end for me if **Adrian** marries **Elisa**? It is certain that my life will become increasingly difficult.

As soon as we reached the **Catania** province, we thought the path was clear for us, but things are going contrary to what we planned. We did not fully appreciate the extent of the hardship that would confront us. I never imagined that one day I would sleep holding my stomach from hunger... Yes, that was after running out of the money we had.

At that time, we had not yet secured a job. Many immigrants portray Europe as a paradise on earth, ignoring the suffering that one faces to earn a living. It is true that the effort is worth the risk because once residency is settled, the immigrant will benefit from all rights like any Italian citizen.

But every expatriate should tell the whole truth to the young people who are about to take on the adventure. It may take a long time to gain all the rights, and the dream may never come true. I regularly speak to my family, telling them that everything is fine, while my true state says otherwise. I felt great relief recently when my father agreed to talk to me after being angry and refusing to speak due to my sudden departure.

On a routine morning, I headed to the market, waiting for it to open. In that state, a person approached me. After recognizing him, I realized he was one of the merchants, **Sheikh Salim**, of Turkish origin. Usually, he would pass by me, greet, and ask about my well-being, but this time I was surprised when he sat in front of me.

He started asking about my conditions and living situation. I felt at ease talking to him from the first moment, especially since my mental state needed such a conversation. I began to tell him what was on my mind, seizing the opportunity to express the distress I was feeling. **Sheikh Salim** asked and listened attentively to everything I said, engaging with everything I narrated. His interest showed me that he cared about the migrants in the area.

Expressing a desire to extend the conversation, he said, "You must be patient, young man. It is good that you are holding on in a country where it is easy to give in to desires. And since you wake up at this early hour, you open a door for livelihood. I understood from your words that you are looking to improve your social situation. In the same context, I came to you to suggest a job offer that might suit you."

I said eagerly, "Go ahead, Sheikh, what is the nature of this job?"

Sheikh Salim smiled and said, "Yesterday, an old friend of mine of Syrian origin named **Irfan** called me. He used to own a restaurant in this area a long time ago but eventually decided to go to the capital, Rome, to develop himself and his business. He now owns a medium-sized restaurant in the city center. He called looking for a trustworthy person in need of work. Personally, I consider you a good and trustworthy person despite my superficial acquaintance with you. You were the first person who came to my mind to offer this opportunity. I don't have more details, but if you are interested, I will inform you of the updates this evening... if you wish, of course."

I welcomed the idea despite my fear of Rome, known for the frequent inspections by police patrols, which could result in administrative deportation if I were caught. Such deportation would be a setback, returning me to square one.

I thanked **Sheikh Salim** and expressed my desire to take the opportunity. This was exactly what I wanted: a life of my own that I would manage myself. Living here in **Adreno** under these conditions, I would be another burden on **Adrian**.

I knew well that he would try to stand in my way, refusing my departure, but it was a good opportunity that I had to seize. Life's opportunities do not come every day; they may come once in a lifetime or never at all. We both dream of obtaining administrative documents that enable us to live like other people in the European Union countries. But each of us must live our predetermined fate.

After calling the restaurant owner and discussing with him, I decided to go and settle in Rome. I found the offer generous compared to my current situation. The offer was for a multi-service position focusing on cleaning and washing dishes, with a wage of six euros per hour and a free meal daily.

Additionally, the job required working full-time for ten hours every day without benefiting from weekly and annual holidays. All this would be done in complete secrecy to avoid penalties since my employment was illegal.

I know well that I am being exploited because I do not have the documents, but since the offer would improve my financial situation, I decided to forgo my current living conditions, which do not even allow me to afford food and rent. Six euros an hour is much less than the standard wage in Italy, but I have no choice that allows me to impose my terms.

Irfan told me about the availability of a small apartment at a reasonable price in the **Labaro** area, which is fourteen kilometers outside Rome. This eased my decision and encouraged me further, especially with the availability of transportation between the place of residence and the workplace.

More than seven months of fatigue and pressure I spent in **Adreno** did not benefit me except for learning the Italian language. I don't even have the money for a ticket to travel to Rome.

What makes me compelled to ask **Adrian** for a loan is that he is better off financially, but I have to convince him of my plan first. Achieving what has been planned for a while depends, at least a little, on my staying by his side and supporting him through hardships. True, we will suffer from loneliness after separation, but I prefer to embark on a new experience that might be the reason for changing my life for the better.

I entered the room where we were staying, which we had arranged in a manner similar to **Adrian**'s room back home. I lay down on my bed and began to recount what I was about to do. **Adrian** expressed his reservations about living in Rome, which is teeming with scammers and swindlers like the mafia groups present in every corner there, unlike the city we currently live in, which is characterized by tranquility and peace, as evidenced by the crime rate that is almost nonexistent.

I leaned on my side and rested my head on my hand and said, "You are like a brother to me. For a while, we have been sharing the sweet and the bitter together. I knew you wouldn't like the idea because I know how you think, but I have grown weary of this miserable life. Sometimes I feel like I'm living like an animal. If it weren't for my faith in fate, I would have gone mad by now. I am going through a difficult period, and you know that better than anyone. What I have gone through in recent months is not easy, and I still haven't gotten over the shock. It's true that staying together gives us both greater strengths, but so far I haven't found the way out that allows me to overcome the incident that broke my back."

Adrian interrupted me, showing a puzzled expression: "What do you mean by shock, are you talking about your relationship with **Maya**? Are you still thinking about her until now?"

I replied with a spirit showing my low morale: "Yes, unfortunately, staying in this city has not distracted me from thinking about her. Every day, her image haunts me in the body of every girl that catches my eye. My desire to forget everything related to her is the main reason that made me agree to migrate. But the excessive calm of this city bridges my heart to sadness and longing. I think I need to live under the pressure and noise of the city... This might be the best solution to divert my thinking towards the future and focus on work and worldly concerns. I will work to improve my living standards and save some money."

Adrian spoke in a low voice: "So that's it, even though I don't approve of your decision, I won't oppose your desire. Since you expressed the wish to take the leap of migration by my side, I have drawn all my future plans with you in them. It will be difficult for both of us to continue living as strangers among people without supporting each other, but it seems that you have made your decision, and that's final. So, all I have left is to wish you good luck and success."

Adrian sighed as he spoke his last words, and his voice leaned towards crying. His words affected me, making me shed tears without warning. I don't remember us crying in front of each other, not before many years when we were little children. I will never forget this night as long as I live. I felt the loss of a brother who is still alive. It's not as easy as it seems. It's a companionship of many long years of life. It's hard to lose someone you found in the settings of your life and can't even remember how the meeting and acquaintance took place.

After a week of arranging and coordinating, a travel date was set. I went to the market on the morning of the departure to thank **Sheikh Salim** who advised me to leave this miserable life.

I headed to the bus station with **Adrian** and **Elisa** to seize the last moments together, which might delay the meeting afterward. We had an emotional farewell, which made me rush to board the bus, unable to bear more emotions and to avoid crying again. I wished the best for my companions and set off towards the unknown to meet my destiny.

Chapter Ten

Two years have passed since my stay in the enchanting city of Rome. A period in which I found psychological comfort I missed in **Adreno**. I didn't feel the weeks and months pass because of continuous work. I find working in the restaurant very enjoyable despite the severe exhaustion it causes me.

The employees have become like family to me due to the excellent treatment I receive from them. I don't recall my skin being as fair as it is now, which is due to not being exposed to sunlight from staying inside the restaurant all day.

After a period of cleaning and washing dishes, the head chef recently allowed me to help in preparing dishes occasionally. I am very happy to discover the world of cooking, which I found to be an unparalleled pleasure.

Despite my endless attempts to neglect my loneliness, I still face solitude and isolation whenever night falls and I enter my dark room. I miss chatting with someone I trust, talking about my thoughts and daily work, my hardships, and dreams.

But the reality is that solitude and isolation are my companions every night. Memories of infatuation that I have not yet forgotten haunt me, and I ask myself if reconnecting with someone would mend my brokenness and stop the recurring visits of events, I have repeatedly wished I could erase from my mind.

Adrian encourages me in every phone call to look for a girl to marry, just as he did with **Elisa** a few months ago. I attended their modest wedding, where the couple announced their marriage without holding a large wedding ceremony with many guests. They planned it that way because **Elisa**'s family still had reservations about their marriage, which made me very happy for my friend and his wife.

Throughout my stay in Rome, I have stayed far from people residing illegally. This was in response to warnings from the restaurant owner **Irfan** regarding young people living under the same conditions as mine, but whose flaw is their engagement in theft, especially at train stations. Many earn their daily bread by working in drug trafficking and buying and selling stolen goods. The strange and puzzling thing is that they describe these dirty deeds as self-reliance and resourcefulness.

I work every day for ten hours, often exceeding ten hours on weekends. My colleagues ask if it is tiring, being the only one working such long hours.

I always reply that the work is exhausting but I prefer staying with those I consider my family over sitting alone at home. I live a comfortable financial situation and enjoy good physical health. I often wonder...

What will become of me and who will take care of me if I get sick? That's why I strive to take care of my body by eating healthy and exercising when I have the time.

I dive into daydreams and ask myself... What if **Maya** were by my side now? What if we lived as husband and wife in the same house I currently reside in? I think about my questions, continuing to daydream... I dream of a beautiful little girl resembling her, whom we alternately care for and protect. We live in happiness and affection that make us want to cling to life. At least I would get rid of the constant hiding from police officers, fearing arrest. With such a family, the authorities might take care of our case and settle our situation. That would be ideal for me.

I come back and wake up from my reverie to find myself every time looking at a mirage with a wistful smile on my lips. Then, I am gripped by the fear of entering a crisis that could drive my mind to madness.

I have become intensely nostalgic for my old life when I was surrounded by people who cared about me without expecting anything in return. I have developed a distrust of people, which has prevented me from forming close friendships despite having some friendly colleagues in my life like the girl **Karina**, who always tries to get close to me.

Karina plays the role of the independent European girl who relies on herself and fights to prove her worth, and she is eager to improve her living standards. We work together cleaning the restaurant and washing dishes. I do the hard work on her behalf due to her inability to handle strenuous tasks as a woman. Meanwhile, I seize the opportunity to tease her for not achieving the equality she believes in and sings about.

We create a fun atmosphere together, which made my friends in the restaurant ask me to date her, citing the beautiful connection between us.

Karina is moderately attractive, characterized by her unique styles, an example being her strange haircuts and dyes that she changes constantly. She always tries to get close to me. Not long ago, I decided to give us both a chance and invited her to have ice cream after work.

We bought the refreshments from a well-known store for the quality of its products. It was my first date with a girl in a long time, and I don't know why I felt very uneasy then. We headed to **Navona Square**, known for its large number of tourists during that time of the year. I began to ponder her pink hair after she sat on one of the public benches near the fountain and asked, "Karina, what does this name mean?"

She answered after she was comfortable in her seat: "I don't really know if it has a meaning or not."

I said, "Very nice... a short and easy-to-remember word."

We were having a friendly and funny conversation, but my uneasiness increased, as if I was lying to myself by dating a girl with whom I had no hope of a positive outcome. It crossed my mind that what I was doing might harm one of us, and it was likely that **Karina** would be the one to get hurt because my heart was still attached to someone else.

I felt guilty just thinking about it, so without warning, I apologized and asked to go home to rest and return to work the next day. Since that day, **Karina** has looked at me as if I were an oddball, the funny thing is that we ended up exchanging the same opinion about each other. But I am truly happy with the way things turned out.

It is said that all roads lead to Rome, and I am fully convinced that all paths would lead to the failure of our relationship.

Today is Saturday, and work pressure is high due to the weekend. **Irfan** asked me to stay and work extra hours. I stayed in the restaurant, engrossed in work until after sunset. It was a tiring day but one that helped me earn extra income to help myself pay bills and rent.

I left through the back door as usual, being an illegal worker. I was surprised by the presence of a significant number of police officers. It seemed something was happening in the suburb. I thought about turning back but realized such a reaction would arouse suspicion.

I decided to walk through them, hoping to evade interrogation. Neither my appearance nor my actions indicated that I was an illegal resident. I hoped that would allow me to pass them safely. I tried to avoid looking at faces, walking with uneasy steps as if I had lost my way. I had never encountered such a situation during my entire stay in Italy.

My anxiety increased when one of the policemen stood in my path and extended his hand in front of my face, signaling me to stop. I thought about running away, but that would be futile given the large number of security personnel in the area.

The officer greeted me and said: "Please, sir, hand me your ID."

I replied, trying to hide my fear after searching my pockets: "I don't have it with me, sir. I must have forgotten it."

The man approached me and asked: "Did you forget it or do you not have an ID?"

I answered: "I forgot it at home, sir."

The policeman spoke after grabbing my wrist: "You need to come with us and call someone to bring the ID."

At that moment, I began to doubt that the journey would end here. Would all this hardship end so easily without any resistance from me?

About two and a half years full of sacrifice and risk would be destroyed this simply.

Being arrested and handcuffed for the first time in my life was the most painful experience. I was put in the police car and taken to the nearest police station.

After hours of waiting, I was brought before an expert in illegal immigration.

He began with the first question: "How old are you?"

I lied, trying to evade: "Seventeen."

I realized then that this answer confirmed to the expert that I was an illegal immigrant. I had passed the age of twenty-seven a few months ago, and looking at my face alone was enough to reveal that.

The man reacted with sarcasm and said: "Okay, we'll verify this after we examine you with the new bone scanner, through which we will approximately determine your age."

After hearing what he said, I thought to myself painfully: "Goodbye, Rome. Goodbye, my dreams. Goodbye, documents. Goodbye..."

He added another question: "Which country are you from?"

I lied once more, trying to save what could be saved. I decided the best solution was to pretend to be caught by the authorities in hopes of gaining political asylum due to the difficult circumstances I was living under.

The expert smiled and asked: "Really?"

I said: "Yes."

The question was enough to render me speechless and unable to speak. I was then taken to one of the cells to await the completion of investigations before being imprisoned.

The bone test result showed twenty-five years. I was taken to **Balbino** prison in the **Rome** province, awaiting the verdict.

I found myself among prisoners of various kinds, including a significant number of illegal immigrants, while the majority were criminals of all sorts, from mafia gangs and drug dealers to thieves and murderers.

I couldn't bear the life of a prisoner who had no place among the wicked. I couldn't believe I was in prison. Sometimes I felt like I was living an experience that wasn't mine, as if I was testing another person's life and after a short while, the role reversal would end, and everything would return to its natural state.

I felt remorse every moment I spent within the dilapidated prison walls. My eyes filled with tears every time I remembered my family, who thought I was in control of the situation. I counted the days with longing for the verdict to be issued as soon as possible. I convinced myself that no matter what form the verdict took, it would be better than remaining detained.

I wasted years of the best days of my life in exile. I reproached myself and felt regret for choosing migration, but the ultimate blame lay with you, **Maya**. You were the main reason that drove me to take on the adventure. I wouldn't have left the homeland if you hadn't abandoned me. I admit I tried hard to achieve a decent living, but erasing you from my memory was my primary and most important goal. How sorry I am for my miserable failure to achieve my goal. You changed the course of my life.

I always thought you would add charm and meaning to my life, but my feeling was wrong this time. I rushed to judgment when I should have listened to those who say wars are measured by their outcomes, not by their horrors and hardships.

I liken my heart to a newly formed coal resulting from the burning of a dry branch. You ignited it and set it ablaze in my unawareness, turning it into an ember. It burned naively to keep you warm and comfort you with its light, while you exhausted its energy, turning it into ash and ending its life.

That was the journey of my heart with you, **Maya**. Coal, then ember, then ash. I don't understand the nature of this love that prevents me from hating you, even though you were the cause of all the pain that threw me into its depths.

The verdict was finally issued after three weeks I spent in prison. The ruling required my departure on the first ship heading home. I was happy with the news as much as I was sad. I was happy to return to my family and loved ones and to get rid of a life of fear and hiding.

I was joyful to breathe the air of freedom after years of hiding and evading. I was pleased to have learned a new language and culture that I wouldn't have discovered without the experience. But I was sad to return empty-handed without achieving my set goals. I was disheartened by the return to memories I wished to forget forever, gloomy about the imprisonment I would face at home according to the law applied to all illegal immigrants.

I would be sentenced to imprisonment for a period ranging from two to six months, with a fine determined by the court.

I was sentenced to three months in prison and a fine of twenty thousand dinars. This period gave me time to think about many things. I would be turning twenty-eight in a few weeks, and things were no longer the same as they were before I left the homeland.

Now the state would treat me like a criminal, which means the job I once dreamed of in government institutions had become an impossible goal, as national companies do not hire individuals with criminal records.

I prepared myself for a difficult life, knowing that even private companies tend to avoid employing those who have been through correctional institutions. However, I believed deep down that I would manage, as I had become accustomed to dealing with tough and challenging situations throughout the past years.

Hope returned to me when I thought of myself as rejected, thanks to the warm reception I received from my family and the neighborhood residents. Everything was perfect. I feared my father's reaction, worrying that he might be upset due to the anger I had caused him.

But in reality, the opposite happened. I received the biggest hug from my father in my entire life, and it was the first time I saw his precious tears since my mother passed away.

Nothing much had changed in my city. Everything was almost as I had left it, except for a new grocery store and a significant change in my brother **Damian**, who had developed a physique much more robust than mine. He would be finishing his studies in a few months.

Now, I had to get used to a new life, completely different from the one I lived before migration. **Adrian**'s absence would make a big difference in my habits. I now had to adhere to always staying at home.

Besides **Damian**, I was pleased to reconnect with my uncle **Gabriel** and aunt **Grace** during a visit filled with emotions. We talked a lot about the beautiful memories we shared, memories that seemed now like a fantasy to recall. We laughed and cried at the same time.

I reassured them about their cherished one, saying he now lived a stable life, free from dangers and problems. I also informed them that he had planned to surprise them with a special visit this year but canceled it after discovering a few days ago that his marriage would result in the birth of a baby after confirming his wife **Elisa** was pregnant.

Adrian's parents were overjoyed. I hadn't known they were unaware of the pregnancy news. I feared I might have spoiled the sweetness of hearing the news from their son. So, I later apologized to **Adrian**, who understood the matter and wasn't upset, but instead, was very happy with my visit to his parents.

I had not yet adjusted to my current situation. I did not know if my new life would remain this way or if it would change after a few days of continuous welcome. Sitting with the neighborhood residents often led to talking about the conditions of exile and migration.

I always garnered attention when recounting the events I had faced. Everyone was interested in hearing those stories. I tried to focus on the negatives more than the positives, especially when seeing those young, bright eyes following with interest and absorbing details, sensing their eagerness to take on the adventure.

I tried to hide the positive aspects to protect them from facing the worst. I always told them that things were very difficult there. Despite my warnings and recounting stories that led their protagonists to ruin, the response was always that **Adrian** had succeeded in settling his civil status and now enjoyed all the rights like any European citizen.

I met many people who were impossible to convince to abandon the idea of migration. Some believed it was a matter of fate and that everyone had to experience their journey in life.

Therefore, every attempt to convince them to give up the idea of migration ended in failure.

It was necessary to live reality anew. Everything and every inch here reminded me of my rosy days with **Maya**. I had to continue with life, hoping to forget with the passage of time, as time alone could heal the wounds of the soul. I realized that it would have been better to refrain from migration from the beginning because, throughout that period abroad, I couldn't forget **Maya** for even a single day.

If the situation continued as it was, I would enter a financial crisis. Therefore, I needed to find a job as soon as possible. I aspired to work with a restaurant given the experience I had gained in cooking.

Sometimes I thought that if I had stayed here and focused on building my future, I would now have a respectable job or perhaps my own project. Then I would return to reality and bear the consequences of my actions, no matter what they were. I had to rebuild my life from scratch and start anew. I decided to look for a job in any field.

My only condition was that the job should provide me with an honest livelihood to maintain my dignity. I announced my need for work to everyone I met, hoping to receive an offer as soon as possible, despite the difficulty due to my tainted criminal record.

Chapter Eleven

Twenty days of idleness, with nothing to do but wander through the city's alleys and occasionally chat with the neighborhood's residents. Today is Friday, so I decided to go to the weekly market, which I had always longed to visit.

I felt immense joy upon seeing that it had retained its old, popular flavor. As I walked and looked right and left to examine the goods displayed on the sidewalks, I suddenly heard a voice calling my name from behind... **Mason, Mason.**

I turned to follow the source of the voice... It was **John**, my former colleague at the fabric warehouse. We had often worked together carrying goods before I moved on to managing the shop. He approached me after navigating through the crowd.

He extended his hands and threw himself in front of me, so I opened my arms to greet him with a hug and a pat on the back. After exchanging words and asking about the latest news, he asked: "And are you currently unemployed?"

I replied: "Yes, I am in search of a job."

He spoke in a serious tone: "I have news that you might be interested in, but it's not suitable to discuss it while we're standing here. Come, I'll invite you for a cup of coffee, and we can talk about it."

We headed to a nearby café and sat down. I focused on every word that came out of **John**'s mouth. From his words, I understood that my uncle **Sebastian** and his son **Caleb** had passed away about three months ago in a car accident in a rural area while returning from visiting a sick relative. This incident led to the shop's closure for a long time, and it only reopened a month ago. However, the business had not returned to its former state.

The shop's closure for two months had caused customers to turn to competing stores, resulting in the shop retaining only two employees due to stagnant goods and declining revenues. Additionally, the task of management had been entrusted to an elderly man with no connection to commerce, whose only relation was that he was the father of **Caleb**'s widow, who inherited the shop and its contents.

John told me that he had mentioned me a few days ago to the elderly man named **Alexander** and informed him about the successful methods **Caleb** and I had adopted in managing the shop. At that point, he inquired about the possibility of contacting me, expressing regret when he learned I was living abroad. **John** asked for my permission to inform the shop owner of my return to the homeland and inquired if I was interested in resuming my former position.

I was deeply saddened by what had happened to **Caleb** and his father. I never expected such an end for them. I had hoped to apologize to my uncle **Sebastian** for leaving the job without informing him of my departure.

I accepted **John**'s proposal without any hesitation, hoping it might be a good omen to open a door for livelihood after others had closed around me.

Two days after that meeting, right after lunch, I was surprised by the ringing of my phone, which rarely rang. I was pleased when I looked at the screen and saw the new number, I had recently added to the call list... It was **John**'s number, who, after greeting me, asked for permission to hand the phone to someone else who wanted to talk to me.

I replied: "Of course, go ahead and give it to him."

A slow, deep voice spoke, indicating it was an elderly man. He mentioned that he had heard a lot about me and was interested in meeting to discuss an important matter regarding a job offer. He also requested that I come to the shop the next morning if I was interested in working with him.

We exchanged words in a friendly manner. I expressed my appreciation for the idea and agreed to the proposed meeting time for the discussion.

I woke up on Monday morning half an hour before the alarm went off, determined to attend the meeting at the specified time. As I saw the shop from a distance, memories of the old days came flooding back. I felt a surge of longing and nostalgia in every part of my body. I received a warm welcome from **John** and my other colleague, **Fedak**, which intensified my feelings of nostalgia and longing.

I noticed that **Alexander** was observing my behavior, wanting to understand my nature and how I interacted with others. We entered the office after exchanging greetings.

He began speaking: "It is clear that you have a good reputation among the workers here. Everyone speaks highly of your work quality and good character. This made me think about working with you. You must have heard what happened to **Sebastian** and his son **Caleb**. Since **Sebastian** has no other son than **Caleb** and since his wife passed away some time ago, my grandson is the sole legal heir to the shop, and my daughter is the custodian until he reaches adulthood.

He added: "Now, at this age, I cannot manage a demanding business like this, especially without having any qualifications in the fabric trade.

Now that the shop has been closed for a long time, concluding deals has become more challenging."

Therefore, after consulting with the current owner of the shop, we thought of seeking your help to restore the business to its former glory. Now, after sharing all this information, I am waiting for your answer regarding whether you would like to take on the challenge.

I was filled with joy at the opportunity presented, but I tried hard to hide my happiness in front of **Alexander**.

I replied with the coolness of a diplomat: "Of course, we can do this together, but we need to proceed with caution and study the market anew. We also need to rely on a list of phone numbers, whether for customers or suppliers."

Alexander interrupted me and said: "How can we get these numbers?"

I said: "Let's not worry about that now. We first need to negotiate how the work will be managed, and then we will chart the path to restoring the business to its previous state and beyond."

Alexander responded: "You are right, my son, but currently we cannot negotiate formally, especially with my daughter's absence. What I propose now is to start working at a suitable wage, and after a month and a half from now, we will arrange a meeting with the shop owner to negotiate based on the results you will achieve. Then, I may leave you with all the management responsibilities by following a work contract that will be between you and the legal custodian."

From the sound of the conversation, it seemed like an invaluable opportunity, but I was worried the elderly man might deceive me and fire me after he learned the intricacies of the business and the trade recovered. Nonetheless, I couldn't refuse such a generous offer as it was the only available option.

I wouldn't lose much from trying; just a month and a half of hard work wouldn't make a difference as long as it would give me a dose of hope to rise again.

I said: "No problem then, but I have one condition if positive results are achieved."

He replied: "What is your condition?"

I said: "We will negotiate later on a percentage of the monthly profits. That will give me additional motivation to work diligently and seriously to achieve incremental results that will benefit everyone. This type of contract is used by many traders in similar cases."

He answered without any hesitation: "Okay, we agree. This is the same idea proposed by the shop owner."

I said: "Alright, I'm in then."

We agreed to start working the day after the meeting. I asked **Alexander** to bring a notebook to transfer the phone numbers from **Caleb**'s phone to reestablish contact with the clients as a first step, whether they were customers or suppliers.

The next day, I contacted all the numbers listed in the notebook, which took me the whole day. I took this step despite knowing it wouldn't yield much in practical terms.

Its purpose was to announce the shop's return to its former state. It was just an advertisement to inform everyone we had dealt with that the fabric shop was back in service and to inform everyone who knew me that I had returned to work.

The customers didn't respond as expected, so I had to move on to the second step, which involved organizing special offers and providing discounts for an entire week with the aim of attracting merchants. It was also necessary to deal with loans for some trusted customers.

After just two weeks of hard work, we recovered about a third of the income that was generated before the accident.

As time passed, everyone noticed the improvement in sales results and the increase in demand for goods, to the extent that the shop regained much of its prestige. After exhausting all my energy as the first to enter the shop and the last to leave, and having to assist in unloading and organizing goods due to a lack of staff, we decided to now restore the actual number of workers in a short period.

Alexander came every day to monitor the improving situation. He usually expressed his admiration for the progress made, but on the other hand, he was very concerned about accounting matters to avoid losses. I understood that he had not yet granted me the necessary trust.

After three weeks of reviewing the old accounts, I discovered something extremely important: a large shipment of goods had been sent to a customer a few months ago, and it was agreed that the amount would be paid within two weeks, but the car accident prevented that.

Apparently, greed had taken over the customer who had hidden the owed amount all this time because the only two men who knew about it had passed away. After informing **Alexander** of the matter, I immediately began to pressure the merchant to recover the hidden funds, which would breathe new life into our business by providing new categories of fabrics and diversifying the options for customers.

This would create the variety the shop was previously known for. After putting significant pressure on the guilty party, even threatening a lawsuit, we recovered the full amount, which was invested in reviving the competitive spirit in our business.

This was the fresh start that allowed the shop to regain its capital and reestablish its reputation in just one month. It was also the opportunity that made **Alexander** appreciate and trust me more and more.

In truth, we achieved results that I personally had not dreamed of. Recovering more than seventy-five percent of the transactions in just one month was beyond the imagination of even the most optimistic after the severe recession the shop had experienced. I am proud of what I have accomplished so far, having done work that everyone attests was challenging to achieve.

After the tremendous success achieved in less than a month and a half, it was time to prepare for the anticipated meeting between me and the shop's custodian in the presence of her father, **Alexander**. We agreed to hold the meeting the next day, Friday, to speak more freely since it was a holiday, and there would be no one else in the shop.

For days I had been preparing what to say during the meeting to persuade the owner to accept my inclusion in the profits at the highest percentage. I deserved it given the results achieved. I aspired to obtain a third of the monthly profits, which would grant me an incredible amount I had never dreamed of throughout my life.

The awaited day arrived, and I was full of hope to seize my golden opportunity—the chance I had crossed the seas searching for, which had been close to me all along. It's really strange how life works, making some people struggle endlessly for ease without bringing them any closer to achieving it, while others don't need to burden themselves to attain wealth and prosperity.

We humans have become accustomed to pursuing and monitoring stability, hoping for eternal happiness, but the truth is that the nature of human beings is built on instability.

I arrived an hour before the agreed time to organize some of the messy items in the storehouse. I noticed a roll of fabric that a customer had moved the previous evening after realizing he didn't have enough money to buy it.

Leaving it on the ground would deteriorate its condition, so I had to move it to ensure proper storage conditions. I carried the roll and carefully climbed the ladder to place it on its designated shelf, about six meters high.

I was alerted by noise indicating the entry of people into the storehouse. I looked back while holding the ladder with one hand and the fabric roll under my other arm. I saw **Alexander** approaching with a woman behind him. Her walk and hurried steps seemed familiar to me.

Her face was covered by the body of her baby that she was carrying. As she talked to her father, her voice pierced my ears, triggering my mind's recognition. What's happening exactly? My heart almost leaped out of its place just by hearing that voice.

The voice got closer with the approaching steps, and her features became clearer. I didn't know what was happening to me; all my senses were collapsing now. The closer she came, the weaker I felt all over my body. Her face began to reveal itself as she approached.

She suddenly stopped walking after glancing at me. The storehouse light now reached her face, refreshing my memory. It was **Maya**—yes, my Snow White. What was she doing here?

All those images rushed back in front of my eyes while my body collapsed from the ladder and the fabric roll slipped from my hand, creating a flying scarf descending towards the ground. My body was falling, and I couldn't control it. I was diving into painful memories of the past while a breeze hit my face. Was I falling? Yes, it seemed so, given the rapid speed with which I was heading towards the ground.

I asked myself in confusion... How could this happen? Could it be that **Maya** was **Caleb**'s widow? No, this is impossible. The events and memories replayed before my eyes like images. Why did I stop at this particular image? An image I could barely recall due to the triviality of the incident. **Caleb** was holding my phone, which I had left on the desk while I went into the hall!

It happened on a routine day, about three weeks after **Caleb** returned. I was sitting in my office when customer traffic decreased, and **Caleb** brought sandwiches for lunch.

I hurried to eat my food quickly to save some time for chatting with **Maya** before the work pace picked up in the evening. I began messaging her while talking to **Caleb** at the same time. He was still eating his sandwich and looking at me with an expression I hadn't seen from him before.

I paid no attention to those strange looks. After a short while, I said goodbye to **Maya** and asked **Caleb** for permission. I put my phone aside and went to take a break, only to be astonished when I returned to find **Caleb** holding my phone with both hands, his sandwich beside him. He froze in place for a moment when he saw me at the door.

I fixed my gaze on him, bewilderment written all over my face. I approached him slowly and said: "What are you doing with my phone? Why are you holding it between your hands?"

He replied after putting it back in place, smiling: "What's wrong with you? Why all this worry?"

He added after picking up his food: "It's just a phone. Why are you so scared? I just wanted to check the time to know the exact hour. I thought my phone's clock was incorrect, but it seems it's working fine."

I was skeptical about the truth of what he said. His demeanor and actions suggested he was lying. But what I couldn't understand at the time was what he was doing with my phone. Was he spying on me? I wondered if I had locked the phone or left it open.

What would he do with my personal information? I asked myself that question repeatedly that day. In the end, I reasoned that he was concerned about his father's resources, which required him to worry about his properties as the sole legal heir.

So, he was trying to spy on and monitor me. Despite all those rationales, I was surprised by the brazen method he used. He should have asked about my reputation among people or set up a prank to test me, as many reasonable people do. No matter what his intention was, this approach was wrong, and I wouldn't allow anyone to check my phone, which was personal and contained private and family matters. When it comes to family, that's a red line that shouldn't be crossed, and I wouldn't forgive anyone for a similar act. But I didn't have enough evidence to accuse him or call him a liar.

Now, the truth dawned on me as I fell. Why hadn't I thought of this scenario back then? Many events would have been clearer if I had realized it. It had never crossed my mind. **Caleb**, you betrayed my trust. That was how you found **Maya**. It was the beginning of a betrayal between a friend and a lover who mastered a game I didn't understand until it was too late.

Chapter Twelve

Where am I? Why am I here? People in white coats, tubes implanted in my body, and all this equipment. Am I in the hospital? I tried to strain myself to sit up but couldn't. A lady, who seemed to be a nurse, noticed my state.

She approached me and said, after placing her hand on my chest to steady me: "Calm yourself, sir. You need to rest after the surgery you underwent following the fall you experienced. You were in a coma for over ten hours, so you must avoid movement to preserve your health."

I tried to speak but to no avail. What happened to my voice? The image of the incident returned to me after the nurse mentioned the fall. The last thing I remembered was my body collapsing from the ladder and approaching the ground. My memory flashed to the last face I saw before my body crumbled, **Maya**'s face, which I always considered angelic. Today, I witnessed the betrayal of those features. Yes, a traitor... I can't describe her with any other title.

I felt as if I were pinned under a heavy cover preventing me from moving. What surprised me was the complete absence of pain. There must be a line connected to my hand supplying a strong anesthetic, making me this comfortable. After a quick glance to inspect my body parts, I found that I had multiple fractures, including a splint on my left hand and a neck brace supporting my neck.

I spent that night in extreme loneliness despite sharing the room with another patient who didn't let a moment pass without releasing sounds of pain, depriving me of sleep all night.

I was thinking about the horrible way I was betrayed by those closest to me, whom I trusted. Despite continuous speculation, I still couldn't grasp what was happening to me, an incident that almost cost me my life. I didn't regain consciousness until I found myself lying on a hospital bed.

At noon the next day, the family was allowed to visit after the doctor announced the stabilization of my condition. I couldn't bear to see my father in that miserable state, especially since I was the reason for his anxiety. When I returned from Italy, I resolved not to upset or cause him distress.

But here I am, doing it again. Despite the prevailing sadness, the visit from my father, accompanied by **Vivian** and **Damian**, restored some balance and spiritual support to my psyche.

However, I couldn't endure the looks of misery on their faces. I tried to communicate with them, but I had no ability to speak. After interacting with exhausted facial expressions, I gestured to **Damian** to bring me paper and a pen to ask some questions. At that moment, the attending doctor entered the room to check on my condition and inform my family about my health status.

He approached me and began inspecting my body parts, noting his observations in his notebook, while my family members watched anxiously.

The doctor spoke and asked my father to follow him to the hallway to talk privately. I sensed something was wrong. I tightly grasped the doctor's coat with my hand connected to the tubes to keep him in the room, eager to hear what he wanted to disclose. The doctor turned towards me, then directly towards my father, as if wanting to hear his opinion on the matter. My father nodded in agreement, giving him the signal to report the results of the examinations in front of everyone.

The doctor began speaking: "After conducting the necessary examinations, it appears that **Mason** has passed the critical stage, and his condition is now stable. The good news is that the head miraculously survived the fall. The success of the surgery performed on the left arm due to varying severity of fractures was confirmed, necessitating the integration of a metal rod in the forearm, with rehabilitation exercises to be performed in a month. Additionally, there is a slight fracture in one of the ribs, which will be easily taken care of."

He paused for a moment, bowing his head as if mustering the courage to announce a piece of news that was difficult for him to articulate.

He spoke after taking a deep breath: "There are some bad news that became clear after the diagnosis. Firstly, regarding the lost voice... This happened due to the throat hitting the edge of the ladder after the fall, causing damage to the neck and throat, which might lead to a permanent loss of voice. However, there is a possibility of gradually recovering it, although the chances of achieving that are very slim. Secondly, concerning the legs... Therefore, I regret to inform you, **Mason**, that you will not be able to stand on your feet again after the damage that occurred to your spinal cord at the pelvic level due to a severe bruise in the spine. Thus, unfortunately, you will spend the rest of your life in a wheelchair with no hope of fixing it."

I couldn't contain myself due to the horror of the news. I tried to get up and scream at the top of my lungs as if trying to prove the doctor's statement wrong, but it was a futile attempt. Both the doctor and my father approached to calm me down.

It seemed my family had heard the news before. I inferred this from their reactions and the sadness that had been etched on their faces since the beginning of the visit. My spirit did not calm until everyone left, and I was alone with my father, who eased my distress with purposeful and logical words that lasted for minutes.

I didn't know how I would continue my life in a wheelchair. Despite the doctors' consensus that the disability would be permanent due to the complete tear in the spinal cord, I couldn't believe I would be unable to walk until days after trying to get out of bed, attempting to move my legs but to no avail. What made matters worse was my inability to speak, but I would try with all my might to regain it, even partially.

I remained in that state between depression and despair at night and regaining hope during the day. Everyone tried to cheer me up and boost my morale to accept the harsh reality. Still, I always asked myself at sunset... Do I deserve all this? What sin did I commit to deserve this punishment?

I spent my fifth day in the hospital under severe psychological distress. Still, I did not have the right to show a moment of weakness in front of the numerous visitors, neighbors, friends, relatives, colleagues, and even people I didn't know. Whether in moments of sorrow or joy, consolation or congratulations bring satisfaction to the person concerned.

After a group of neighborhood residents left and ten minutes before the end of visiting hours, I was surprised by **Maya** entering hesitantly, holding flowers in her hands.

She was the last person I expected to see. I intensely desired to rise from my place and push her out of the room... but alas, I didn't even have the strength to scream at her. I could only write on the notebook beside me or gesture with my bare hand, discolored from the many needle punctures.

But suddenly, a strange desire to hear what she had to say arose within me. She advanced, still in her nervous state. It seemed she had been waiting outside for some time, walking towards me with heavy steps, her eyes never leaving my face.

I immediately turned my gaze towards the ceiling, expressing my disdain. She placed the flowers on the nearby table, her gaze fixed on me. She sat down very slowly, fearing my reaction. Silence prevailed for nearly a minute as I continued to ignore her.

She broke the silence, saying: "I'm not here to ask for your forgiveness, as I don't deserve it. I came to clarify some things that might seem confusing. First, I'm sorry for how things turned out. I heard you won't be able to walk again and that you can't speak either. I witnessed your terrible fall, and I'm grateful you are still alive. I'm aware of everything you've been through over the past years.

It's true that I left you for money. I was a victim of my greed. I left you to be with someone who had status and wealth. But I didn't know you worked in the same shop with **Caleb**. I didn't know you knew each other. I realized that after seeing you a few days ago. I met **Caleb** through social media after his repeated attempts to catch my attention. I eventually gave in and talked to him, leading to a meeting that resulted in mutual—or rather, imaginary—admiration.

I was attracted to his financial capabilities, which you didn't have. So, I thought about taking my time and considering the engagement. I didn't have the courage to be honest with you about the reason for my decision to leave you. I knew very well the pain I was causing you.

A few months after our separation, **Caleb** proposed to me without ever mentioning his knowledge of our relationship or his friendship with you. We got married about six months later. At the beginning of the marriage, everything was great, but as time passed, it became clear that **Caleb** wasn't the person I had always dreamed of. He always got angry over trivial matters, turning everything special into a nightmare. We were on the verge of divorce, but my pregnancy saved it. I decided to sacrifice my happiness for my child's future.

I used to think and ask myself: What if I had married you instead of **Caleb**? You always occupied my mind during that period. One day, as the baby's birth approached, I suggested a name for the boy to **Caleb**. The name I proposed was **Mason**. **Caleb** vehemently opposed it and decided to name the child **Steve**. His rage began that day, and he started treating me with contempt, even resorting to violence on more than one occasion. I should have realized that all that hatred was because of the name. How did I not notice that you two were friends?"

A hospital worker enters to ask visitors to leave the rooms.

She added, after standing up, ready to leave: "For your information, I couldn't forget you all this time. Leaving you was the greatest sin I committed against both of us. I know how kind and pure-hearted you are, so I retract my earlier words and sincerely ask for your forgiveness."

She left hurriedly, leaving my eyes drowning in tears. Life is harsh, but humans create its harshness. I can't deny my pity for **Maya**, but she is now reaping what she sowed. Everything that happened and is happening to her is because of a selfish decision she made herself.

On the other hand, my mistake was being attached to and loving her more than anything else. I paid a high price for that. After hearing everything **Maya** said, I'm unsure whether I can forgive her. After being certain I couldn't forgive her, I now know and am convinced that despite everything that happened, I can't hate her. Yet, I still love her and am madly in love with her...

The End